The Secrets
We Keep

Divyata
Rajaram

INDIA • SINGAPORE • MALAYSIA

ISBN

Paperback 979-8-89929-894-3
Hardcase 979-8-89984-916-9

Contents

Contents

Prologue

The dust had settled, or so they thought. Dubai, with its relentless sun and shimmering facade, had swallowed the secrets whole—secrets of betrayal and loss, secrets that once bound five women together in a web of friendship and deceit.

Dipika is gone forever. Her absence was a constant ache, a reminder of the price they had all paid.

Sakina is back! Vulnerable, after her return from exile in London and desperate to carve a new identity for herself, she yearns for acceptance after emerging from the scandal that destroyed her husband Adil and herself.

Rupali seeks a deeper connection with her dashing husband Rohit Jahangir, the echoes of the past still haunting her waking hours. Planning their only daughter Anisha's wedding will give her renewed purpose.

Anjali, ever the pragmatist, has thrown herself into her work, building an empire on the ashes of shattered trust. Scarred but unyielding, she secretly yearns for love, but will she be successful in navigating the treacherous currents of high society?

Naina is the fragile beauty with a head for business, largely ignored by her business magnate father. She will do anything to climb the ladder of corporate success and protect her family legacy, even if it is from her own husband.

But the desert whispers, and the city never forgets. Just when they believe they have outrun their past, a new shadow stretches across the glittering skyline. A whisper of a name, a familiar face in an unfamiliar place, a chilling echo of the events that had torn their world apart. The women are about to learn that some secrets refuse to stay buried, and that the bonds they thought were severed can be twisted into something far more sinister.

The game, it seems, was never truly over. It had merely paused, awaiting the opportune moment to resume with even higher stakes. And this time, the players are about to discover that the deadliest secrets are not the ones they hide from each other, but the ones they keep from themselves.

Chapter 1

Sakina wearily opened her eyes to the four large grey suitcases currently occupying almost half of the tiny bedroom in the serviced apartment that was now her new residence in Dubai.

Her head felt heavy from a combination of jet lag coupled with lack of sleep. It was hard to sleep through the night. The sounds of the city seeped through the thin walls: the distant wail of sirens, the angry shouts of a late-night argument, the mournful cry of a stray cat. These sounds, along with the pervasive air of neglect and decay, created an atmosphere of unease and foreboding that overwhelmed her.

As she ventured outside the bedroom, she stepped gingerly over a pile of clothes lying on the floor. The air in the apartment hung heavy, thick with the scent of stale cigarette smoke. The peeling wallpaper, a sickly shade of yellow, flaked off in ragged strips, revealing patches of bare plaster. The ceiling, a patchwork of cracks and discoloration, threatened to collapse at any moment. A single, flickering fluorescent bulb cast an eerie glow over the room, illuminating the chipped paint on the furniture and the grime that clung to the edges of the worn-out sofa. There even appeared to be layers of dust on the faded brown carpeting on the floor.

This apartment was clearly a refuge for the forgotten, a place where the weight of poverty and despair settled like a shroud. It was a stark reminder of the harsh realities faced by those living on the margins of society.

She shuddered at the thought that maybe.. just maybe they were here for the long haul.

It was a far cry from what she had imagined to be the homecoming of her dreams.

"Adil…where are you *Jaan*" she called out to her husband. The silence in the apartment was more than she could bear.

"I'll be out soon …I'm in the loo," he replied.

At least she wasn't alone here, she thought, straightening the bed covers and trying to get her thoughts in order. Several pieces of the life she had so carefully constructed in Dubai now lay fragmented before her. She would have to rearrange them carefully and rediscover herself in the process. "Had anyone truly missed them at all?" she wondered.

Over the past two years in London, since they left in ignominy, her emotions had swung from passive acceptance of the circumstances to fury at how her husband's actions had resulted in their exile from the city she had enjoyed living in for so many years. Of course, he had apologised countless times and told her they would resurrect themselves on their return. She desperately wanted to believe him, but knew that the years of being away from Dubai and the crisis they had undergone had taken a huge toll on both of them. Far from being the cool, suave and level-headed senior investment banker that Adil had once been, he was now a pot-bellied, greying, nervous man growing increasingly anxious about the future.

Financial crimes were viewed extremely seriously in Dubai, and Sakina knew they were very lucky to be back in the city at all. Adil had been told very clearly by his previous employers, the powerful ABQ bank, that he would have to lie low until they identified a suitable role for him. Once a professional who'd had his pick of several meaty career opportunities across the globe, he would now have no choice but to wait.. something he had gotten accustomed to over the past two years in London. "Life in the slow lane is good for the health", he would joke with Sakina. She failed to see any humour in the situation.

They now sat across each other at the little square dining table in the apartment in tenuous silence, each waiting for the other to speak. An uncomfortable pause was created by the unusual circumstances they found themselves in. How did one find a way to start over?

Adil's pyjamas, rumpled and stained with coffee, hung loosely on his frame, a testament to sleepless nights and relentless stress. His eyes, bloodshot and bleary, darted across the spreadsheet on his laptop, a maze of numbers blurring into meaningless patterns.

"There has to be a way…," he muttered, his voice hoarse, the words barely audible. His reputation, once pristine, now lay in tatters, smeared with accusations of financial fraud.

He ran a trembling hand through his thinning hair, the weight of the accusations pressing down on him like a physical burden. It felt even worse now that they were back in Dubai and there was no escaping those difficult memories that came flooding back.

He had built his career on integrity, on the unwavering belief that numbers told a story of trust. Those same numbers had been used to paint him as a criminal.

He remembered the whispers, the sidelong glances, the cold, accusatory stares that followed him everywhere. The doors that once swung open for him in Dubai were now firmly shut, the handshakes that once conveyed respect now withdrawn in suspicion. He was an outcast, a pariah, his name synonymous with deceit.

"So what's your plan for the day, Jaan?" he asked, finally peering over the top of his newly acquired rimless glasses at his wife.

Even at this hour of the morning, his wife was a sultry siren. Her skin luminous and her thick henna tinted reddish-brown hair glossy as it tumbled around her shoulders in sleep tousled waves. Her deep brown eyes stared unblinkingly at him. "Shouldn't I be asking you that instead?"

For years, he had played the role of the provider, ensuring that his wife lacked nothing in comforts and luxuries. Her every wish was his command. There he was, the rock-solid husband and banking ace who commanded respect and admiration from every segment of the classy social and business circles they had once belonged to.

Adil's ascent to the apex of the financial world had been as sharp as the Dubai sun that glinted off the sleek glass of the Burj Khalifa, their erstwhile home. His life was a carefully curated tableau of success, each day a testament to his sharp intellect and relentless drive in the high-stakes realm of investment banking. His fully expensed apartment, perched high within the iconic tower, offered breathtaking panoramic views of the sprawling cityscape and the shimmering Arabian Gulf – a constant, dazzling backdrop to his extraordinary life.

Mornings would often begin with a leisurely breakfast prepared by his live-in staff, the aroma of exotic fruits and freshly brewed coffee filling the air. Then, it was a seamless transition into the demanding world of finance, his days a whirlwind of high-powered meetings, multi-million dollar deals, and strategic negotiations conducted from his corner office in the Dubai International Financial Centre. The corporate perks were as lavish as the city itself: chauffeured cars whisking him to appointments, exclusive access to VIP lounges, and a seemingly endless stream of invitations to the city's most glamorous events.

Evenings were a kaleidoscope of glittering parties and exclusive gatherings. Adil and Sakina would effortlessly navigate through throngs of Dubai's elite, champagne flutes in hand, engaging in witty banter and forging invaluable connections. Adil's social calendar was a testament to his status, from rooftop soirees overlooking the Palm Jumeirah to private yacht parties cutting through the moonlit waters.

Luxury was not just a concept; it was the very fabric of his existence. Bespoke suits hung in his walk-in closet, waiting to be chosen for the day's engagements. Rare watches adorned his wrist, each a miniature masterpiece of craftsmanship. His apartment showcased modern design, filled with curated art and the latest technology, a sanctuary of opulence high above the bustling city.

Servants attended to his every need, ensuring that their lives flowed with effortless ease. From maintaining the impeccably clean apartment to preparing gourmet meals at a moment's notice, their discreet efficiency was a silent testament to Adil's wealth.

Yet, amidst this whirlwind of extravagance, there were moments of quiet contemplation within the luxurious confines of his sky-high abode. As the city lights twinkled below, mirroring the stars above, Adil sometimes paused, a fleeting thought perhaps crossing his mind about the true cost of such a life. But the allure of success, the thrill of the deal, and the intoxicating embrace of Dubai's high life would invariably draw him back into its glittering orbit, another day dawning with the promise of further triumphs and the endless possibilities that wealth so effortlessly provided.

And then abruptly, it had all gone so horribly wrong. Everything had changed over the past two years.

Now he could barely remember the events of the day before. The interrogation clouded his mind, the various secrets he had been told to keep silent about. He wanted so much to clear his own name amongst the very banking circles he had worked all his life to gain respect in. And yet, he had been reduced overnight to a complete non-entity and quickly shuffled away to an unknown location and then to London. Organisations were bigger than people; no matter how many lives and identities perished, there was always a bigger picture, and the stakes were high. The company's brand name and reputation could never be compromised. His own personal reputation, of course, lay in tatters, but that was just collateral damage.

For a man who had chased money all his life, Adil had recently accepted that even his own peace of mind was too expensive for him to afford.

" Err…I have a few calls to make, *Jaan*…I want to get back in touch with," he muttered nervously, unable to meet Sakina's accusatory gaze. God forbid she should find out that the day involved completing his journal entries and, of course, the Crossword and Sudoku after the newspaper was delivered.

Sakina could never know what the endless days in a darkened cell at the London headquarters of the Specialist Fraud Division had done to her husband. They had been aggressive and relentless in their questioning, refusing to believe that he was himself a pawn in a much bigger game— simply a victim of circumstances.

With his impressive professional track record and seniority within ABQ bank, surely he knew far more than he had revealed.

After what seemed like endless months of investigative-style questioning, Adil was abruptly released from judicial custody. His many calls to his mentor, Ali Rez, after his release went unanswered. Eventually, when the air tickets to Dubai were mysteriously dropped off at their London apartment, Adil understood that it was now time to go home.

Several questions that he had would have to remain unanswered for now.

Perhaps the worst torture of all, though, was how the wife he had cherished and adored for so many years was now treating him. Respect and admiration in her eyes were replaced by scorn and disregard for anything he ever said. A complete lack of trust in his ability to keep them safe.

He knew how much she blamed him for their current situation – for the humiliation she too had to face in Dubai of all places. The city she loved and the friends she had lorded it over at one point in time. Sexy, funny, scintillating Sakina – the life of every party in tinsel town.

Their 20th wedding anniversary was coming up in a few months time. Adil feared that it maybe their last and Sakina would eventually divorce him.

This had been the status of their relationship for quite some time now. She was the silent predator, and he was the hunted. He sought to avoid a direct conversation with the woman he still loved most of all. There was nothing left to say.

Sakina truly seemed on the brink of pursuing her own fortune and future now that they were back in Dubai. How could he stop her? The girls...her friends in Dubai – Rupali and Anjali were the only ones who had stayed in contact with her right through their ordeal. He knew they would do anything for his wife and hated him for all the distress he had caused her.

Watching Adil's evasiveness made Sakina feel ill. She ignored him at the breakfast table as she mentally made her own plans for the day. Of course Adil was in constant denial of their circumstances and as usual it was her who had to goad him into any kind of action – it was exhausting.

She desperately wanted to contact Rohit, her friend Rupali's husband, even if it was just to have him understand and sympathise with her plight. But she knew it was too dangerous.

She couldn't risk losing Rupali's friendship, especially now that they were back in Dubai. She had been the nicest to her over the past year and Sakina felt terribly guilty for any attraction she felt previously toward Rohit. She couldn't revisit that drama again and risk the friendship.

Besides, constantly stalking their Instagram during her days in exile had clearly depicted their picture-perfect lives in technicolour. Holidays in Rome, Jaunts to the USA to visit their only daughter Anisha, Shopping sprees in Paris where Rupali proudly showed off her Bulgari high jewellery necklace – a gift from her adoring husband Rohit, it had all left Sakina with a deep and brooding sense of discontentment that hung in a constant cloud around her. It was just not fair!

This could have been her life – she had been that close to finding a connection with Rohit. Surely she hadn't imagined the chemistry they had shared, the intense smouldering looks he would give her across a crowded room. The thought of it gave her an exciting tingle down her spine even now – Rohit Jahangir was the ultimate Adonis. Tall, virile and sexy to the core with an easy confidence and a great sense of humour. Of course, it helped that he was a hugely successful business magnate in the music industry too. How wonderful it must be to live a life as Rohit's wife amidst the glitterati of Dubai!

The incessant ringing of the doorbell interrupted her thoughts as she got up to let the sullen faced cleaner in. They could only afford to have her come in twice a week and Sakina wanted to ensure she got her money's worth. The woman looked at her defiantly, expecting resistance as she stated she would only do the surface cleaning in the kitchen, she wouldn't do the dishes and the balcony area was out of bounds.

Sakina was in no mood for a confrontation though and meekly shook her head agreeing to her terms as she showed her where the vacuum cleaner was. Beggars can't be choosers.. it was true, but she wouldn't be a beggar for long.

Adil was infuriatingly still in his pyjamas, mulling over the newspaper that the maid had carried in. Rather than yell at him, Sakina took a deep breath and went to get ready for her own shower. She carefully took out the one Salvatore Ferragamo monogram dress she owned in deep blue. She had sneakily acquired it from an outlet mall in Wembley before they left for Dubai.

She had to get ready to face the outside world, and even if she didn't feel it, it was important to let her friends know she was back!

Chapter 2

Anjali Sen sat in her corner office in the Palm Jumeirah and stared out at the view of the blue expanse of ocean in front of her. She felt a strange sense of uneasiness as she thought about her friends. They had painstakingly pieced their lives back together after the previous year's devastating events, the most painful being their dearest Dipika's demise under such harrowing circumstances. Anjali, in particular, had wrestled with the aftermath, endlessly replaying their shared past, searching for a misstep. How could it have gone so wrong? They had been five vibrant, ambitious women, determined to conquer the world. Dubai, the city of dreams, had been their playground, filled with countless shared moments. They were the epitome of perfection, icons within Dubai's elite circles—wealthy, elegant, and living lives that seemed like a fairy tale.

"Was it as perfect as they had once imagined, though?"– Anjali wondered. Clearly not!

Their lives had come crumbling down in the span of a few months. The edifice of their friendship that she had thought was based on faith, trust, and genuine care for each other turned out to be false and pretentious. Perhaps it had always been this way, and she hadn't wanted to see it for what it truly was. Detective Razi Shufa had certainly opened her eyes to many home truths after their dear friend died. How much the past year had changed them all, she ruminated as she thought about the day ahead.

Anjali had asked Sakina to meet her for lunch. She had no choice but to make her feel welcome now they were back in town. Adil's insider trading and fraudulent activity had left him a complete professional and social outcast. The poor guy had literally nowhere to go and no one to turn to.

At least she could extend her support to Sakina and see what she could do for her. Isn't that what good friends do? Anjali hoped to convince Sakina to get back to working on her own. They could no longer afford to live the luxurious life in Dubai if they had zero income. She knew that the exorbitant legal expenses of clearing Adil's name had burned a big hole in the couple's finances. It was best that she give Sakina a reality check as gently as possible.

Stretching her long legs under her work desk, Anjali pushed her reading glasses up on her head. Somehow, Sakina and trouble always went hand in hand. She wondered if she had changed her flirtatious ways. There was only one way to find out, and that's just what she planned to do.

Anjali was exhausted from being the glue that held all her female friendships together. Her busy professional life as editorial Chief of Dubai Glam left her with precious little time to engage emotionally with anything or anyone outside of work. Yet she had invested a whole lot of her life into cultivating the friendships that were now family to her in many ways. Somewhere, though, her personal life was still bereft of any significant relationship.

Stunningly attractive with her tall, lithe figure and striking looks, Anjali knew she would have no dearth of male admirers if she paid them any attention at all.

And yet, what she yearned for was not just a boyfriend but a soul mate …someone who got her and what she was really like. At 40, she was tired of being single.

"Anjali …I can finish that Paris fashion week summary piece for you if you're planning to leave early today," Tarun, the Art Director of Dubai Glam, popped his head into her office, looking quizzically at her. He could see that Anjali seemed very preoccupied this morning.

As the supremely talented Editorial head of Dubai Glam, the foremost fashion and lifestyle magazine in Dubai, she was lucky to have the best team ever at work. They worked together in brilliant collaboration, ensuring that they never missed any deadlines and always managed to keep every issue of the magazine brimming with fantastic content that their readers were addicted to.

"Thanks Tarun. I'm almost done and just about heading out now. I have a friend who's back in town after a very long while!"

Within the next twenty minutes, she'd snatched her worn leather jacket and the Range Rover Evoque keys and made it swiftly to the building's exit as her head swirled with thoughts.

Meeting Sakina again was crucial. They all needed a clean break from the past year's chaos. Dipika's absence was now a stark reality and one they had all painfully learned to accept. Rupali and Anjali's bond had solidified since then, an unshakeable alliance, formed in the wake of tragic circumstances and the departure of Sakina from Dubai. Amidst that, there had been Sakina's brief dalliance with Rohit, Rupali's husband. How could Anjali ever forget that! Of course, he was to blame as well, but Sakina should have known better. Anjali wouldn't tolerate any further harm to Rupali. Sakina had to understand: their boundaries were absolute. Her unpredictable, tempestuous behaviour was Anjali's primary concern.

They had agreed to meet at Café Mono, a hidden gem in Jumeirah. It was a lush, vibrant restaurant that had recently opened. Anjali chose its secluded ambience to shield Sakina from prying eyes eager to inquire about her abrupt departure from Dubai.

She sipped her guava-infused Triple Sec margarita as she waited for Sakina in the restaurant, and the alcohol was a necessary catalyst for her thoughts. Had she erred in keeping this initial meeting from Rupali? Rupali, ever the loyal friend, had inquired about their group reunion, eager to help Sakina settle back in. Yet, Anjali knew this preliminary conversation with Sakina was essential. Rupali was unaware of certain complexities, which had to remain hidden for now.

A hush fell over the restaurant as Sakina entered, a vision in a flowing, deep blue silk dress that shimmered with each graceful step. The deep sapphire hue accentuated the rich warmth of her skin, and the muted gold embroidery caught the soft glow of the restaurant's lighting, creating a halo around her. Her dark hair, thick and lustrous, cascaded down her back, a stark contrast to the delicate jewellery that adorned her ears and neck.

Her eyes, large and expressive, held a captivating depth, their gaze sweeping across the room with a quiet confidence. A subtle, captivating fragrance, a blend of sandalwood and jasmine, drifted in her wake, further drawing attention. Her lips, full and perfectly shaped, held a hint of a smile, a silent acknowledgement of the attention she commanded.

Heads turned, conversations paused, and silverware stilled as she moved through the room, a magnetic presence that commanded admiration. Each step was a study in elegance, her movements fluid and poised. Far from looking like a victim of difficult circumstances, she was now a stunning woman ready to take on the world. Suddenly, everyone's head had turned to look at the beautiful woman who had just walked in.

"My darling …Anju...how are you?" Sakina gushed warmly, genuinely happy to see Anjali again. Over the past years, Anjali had been Sakina's steady voice of reason, a guiding force even when Sakina resisted. As they embraced, a familiar pang of guilt gnawed at Sakina; she couldn't offer Anjali complete honesty, the truth was too perilous. So much had changed.

"It's wonderful to have you back, babe," Anjali said warmly, rising from her seat to give her friend a warm hug. She had genuinely missed her.

"It's wonderful to be back, Anju. You look amazing."

As the two women exchanged pleasantries and general Dubai news, Anjali studied Sakina across the table. Her expert makeup hadn't fully masked the dark circles under her eyes, and the strain was evident.

"I think I'll have that margarita too, Anju...it looks great. What a lovely place. Great choice!" Sakina said, looking around as she took note of Anjali's subtle concern. She knew she couldn't easily feign normalcy, and so she attempted to change or deflect the conversation.

"So, what's the Dubai buzz? Has Rakesh been in touch? Have you visited HER?" Her eyes widened in alarm as she whispered this last part to Anjali. Their erstwhile friends had certainly created enough turbulence in all their lives.

"Not really" ...said Anjali in a soft voice. Despite the weight of the unspoken questions, Anjali resolved to set them aside. Sakina's well-being and smooth reintegration into their circle took precedence. Everything else could wait.

They ordered drinks and the Primavera pasta, touted as the house speciality. Anjali watched Sakina meticulously list her allergies to their waiter and enquire about multigrain pasta and the freshness of the salad greens.

This new Sakina felt...false, pretentious, like a delicate porcelain doll carefully placed on a shelf, afraid to make a sound or a wrong move. Anjali found herself missing the vibrant chaos that used to surround her friend. She longed for the Sakina who would burst into a room with a hearty greeting, her colourful kurtis starkly contrasting with the muted palettes favoured here.

As Sakina spoke of the Art auctions she had visited in London, her gestures refined and her accent subtly altered, Anjali couldn't reconcile this polished persona with the girl who had once haggled fiercely for bangles in the Gold Souk and devoured spicy biryani with gusto in Deira, her fingers stained with turmeric.

A wave of longing washed over Anjali. She missed the authenticity, the unvarnished truth of her Desi friend from Hyderabad. She missed the loud, boisterous Sakina Nawaz, who wore her heart on her sleeve, whose emotions were as vibrant and untamed as the city she originally came from. This carefully curated elegance felt like a cage, stifling the very essence of the woman Anjali had grown to love. She wanted to shake this new Sakina, to peel back the layers of sophistication and find the familiar, fiery spirit underneath. She yearned for the return of the rustic charmer, the one who was unapologetically herself, flaws and all.

As Sakina carefully examined the Dijon mustard, Anjali softly asked, "How's Adil?

"He's doing okay, yaar. He's setting up meetings, etc., with all his old contacts. The bank has said he can revive his LinkedIn as well and offered to pay for an image consultant to help him resurrect his professional self. It's amazing that his phone hasn't stopped ringing since we got back, Anju."

I hadn't realised how many friends Adil has in Dubai.

"Even I hadn't realised how well you can lie", mused Anjali silently.

"That's amazing", she said out loud, staring at Sakina and truly seeing her for the first time.

Behind the glitz and the glamour, here was a woman who was still determined to defend her husband against all odds. Both of them knew that Adil had very few friends left and even those still in his network had fallen off the radar since they heard the news of his forced exit from ABQ bank.

The professional circles in Dubai were rife with whispers about who was on the take and how much money Adil had made defrauding the bank. His reputation lay in tatters and it was too risky being associated with him.

"Sounds like he'll have no problem at all settling back into a comfortable work routine", Anjali said, lying through her teeth. " He's such a brilliant guy – he won't need much time at all."

Sakina happily agreed as she took her first mouthful of the delicious Primavera pasta. It was delicious! They rarely ate out these days, and it was just wonderful to be lunching out with her friend in Dubai as they did in the good old days. Of course she knew Anjali would offer to pay for lunch.

None of Sakina's credit cards had any balance available, and Adil was keeping her on a tight shoestring budget – something that was painful, especially for someone who was so accustomed to filling every void in her life with retail therapy.

Her phone was now angrily buzzing in vibration mode, and as Sakina looked at it, she froze.

Would the bastard not give her even 48 hrs before he tracked her down? Her stomach began to churn even as she knew Anjali had realised something was amiss.

She would take care of things herself, she thought as she forced a smile on her face and quickly typed a terse message..." Out at lunch. I'll call you as soon as I'm done"

Chapter 3

Rupali, her cheeks glowing with elation, ended the call she was on with Anisha, their daughter in New York. She had now apparently found someone special to share her life with, and her mother was thrilled to hear this news! After their daughter's terrifying encounter with a stalker during her final year of university, Rupali and Rohit had been very worried about her. Although Anisha had since graduated and built a thriving career at a renowned investment bank, there was no denying the lingering trauma the experience had caused.

Anisha's visits to Dubai had become increasingly rare these days, focused as she was on establishing her life in the US. Perhaps, at last, they had a reason for a grand celebration and one that would bring their baby girl home.

Rupali hurried to Rohit's study, where her husband had retreated after dinner in his usual routine, a cigar and a small glass of Chartreuse in hand.

"Ro...it was Anisha," she announced, bursting into the room elated. "It sounds like she's serious about this boyfriend."

The study was Rohit's sanctuary of leather and polished wood, the air thick with the scent of old books and pipe tobacco. He sat in a high-backed leather chair, the dim light from a brass lamp casting sharp angles across his face. His strong and aquiline profile was etched in concentration as he absorbed the words on the pages of the company annual report before him. A thick, dark brow furrowed slightly, emphasising the intensity of his gaze.

He exuded a quiet, undeniable masculinity. It wasn't the boisterous, attention-grabbing kind, but a deep, resonant strength that emanated from within. The set of his jaw, the unwavering focus in his eyes, the sheer stillness of his presence spoke of a man comfortable in his own skin, a man of intellect and quiet power. His hands, large and capable, turned the pages with a quiet authority, the subtle flexing of his forearms visible beneath the rolled-up sleeves of his crisp white shirt. The shirt strained slightly across his broad shoulders and chest, hinting at the powerful physique beneath.

The aura of this room, with its shelves of well-worn books, globes, and antique maps, reflected Rohit's character: a blend of intellect, worldliness, and a touch of the old-fashioned. He was a man who commanded respect without demanding it, his presence filling the room with a palpable sense of masculine energy.

A successful man, made so by his own vision, driving ambition and hard work. In a modern-day Mills and Boon setting, Rupali still saw Rohit as her ultimate man. He now looked up from the report he was reading and smiled. That smile that still made women go weak in the knees, and his own wife was no exception.

Who.... Karan? Rohit was aware that Anisha had been dating her friend from university for the past few months. He just hadn't realised they would decide to take things forward so seriously this soon.

Chalo, he was glad she had figured it out. One less thing to stress out about. He had been extremely worried about his daughter recently.

Anisha had certainly been through a lot at her young age - badly rattled by a past boyfriend's harassment and stalker like behaviour. He had been persistent in pursuing her even after she had told him categorically she wasn't interested. - It had started subtly at first - a bouquet of roses left on her doorstep, a text message with a line from a poem, his unwelcome presence outside her lecture hall. And then his obsession suddenly escalated.

She'd changed her route to class, avoided her usual coffee shop, and even asked her roommate to walk her back to their dorm at night. The constant feeling of being watched, of being followed, was a suffocating weight on Anisha. Her once bright eyes, usually sparkling with laughter and curiosity, were now shadowed with worry, constantly darting around, searching for a familiar, unwelcome presence. Rupali and Rohit were horrified to hear from Anisha about what she was going through, and that too thousands of miles away from their safe haven in Dubai. They knew that she had casually dated this boy in the past but that still did not justify his possessive and cloying behaviour.

And yet, when they contacted Campus Security and even local law enforcement authorities in Boston, they were informed that unless the student made a direct threat to Anisha, there was nothing anyone could do. The situation finally resolved itself when Anisha graduated from college and, thankfully, was able to distance herself from the individual who was harassing her.

Unfortunately, the whole experience had greatly shaken her confidence and caused her to doubt herself and every man around her for several months.

Despite her parents' constant love and reassurance, she had become terrified of close relationships with men. Despite Rupali's gentle suggestion to talk to a professional counsellor, she had staunchly refused. Instead, Anisha had dived headlong into her work, single-mindedly focusing on building a career in investment banking. Late hours at work and almost no social life were now her daily regimen.

When Karan, a former classmate from university, moved to New York, it seemed like the perfect antidote to her relationship woes. They had always been good friends, and Anisha was grateful to have someone she could finally trust to hang out with.

She had known him since their Sophomore year at college, an easy breezy, confident guy. They were a study in contrasts, yet perfectly intertwined. He, a lanky architecture student with perpetually ink-stained fingers and a mop of unruly brown hair, always seemed to be sketching something – a building, a tree, the curve of her smile. She was a vibrant Economics major with a cascade of light brown curls and a laugh that could fill a lecture hall. Having met over a busy mid-term week one semester, they were quick to connect. Their initial dates were casual, a whirlwind of intellectual banter and shared passions. And then gradually, despite their initial attraction to each other over the four-year course, they had somehow drifted apart as they both went on to pursue their post-graduate studies in different states.

A wide smile had bloomed on Anisha's face as she scrolled through Karan's message. "Back in the city!" it read, followed by an invitation for coffee. A warmth spread through her chest, chasing away the familiar chill of another long day survived in the relentless New York grind.

Unexpectedly, Karan reappeared in Anisha's life. He had recently joined a prominent architecture and design firm in Manhattan, and upon reaching out to his old friend, they quickly rekindled their connection, this time forging a more profound bond.

Anisha found herself looking forward to their coffee date with an unusual lightness. It wasn't about romantic rekindling or the pressure of a new relationship. It was about the simple joy of reconnecting with a kindred spirit, someone who knew her before the long hours and the solitary takeout dinners became the norm. In the bustling, often impersonal landscape of New York, Karan's return felt like a welcome reminder of shared laughter, easy conversation, and the comforting embrace of a familiar friendship. It was a lifeline to a past filled with warmth and connection, a promise of genuine human interaction in her present.

Karan was equally delighted to have Anisha back in his life, even more gorgeous than he remembered her to be. She wasn't a new acquaintance requiring careful navigation or a demanding friend needing constant attention. She was familiar, comfortable, and already knew a significant part of his past. There was a shared history, a foundation of understanding that bypassed the awkwardness of first encounters. They were each other's muse, confidante and best friend, and their love story was just beginning to unfold.

Rupali and Rohit were eager to meet Karan in person, even though they had connected briefly on Zoom calls. He appeared to be a handsome, ambitious young man, focused on his career goals. Anisha also shared that his family was wealthy and well-established in London.

"I'm sure Dad will be delighted with that part", she had joked with her mother in private.

Rupali now informed her husband that their daughter was now suggesting a summer trip to London, a chance for both families to meet and solidify their relationship now that Karan had formally proposed. Rohit and she would also fly in, making it a joyous reunion.

"Sounds like a fabulous idea, my dear!"

Rohit was quick to approve, even though they had yet to meet the Rawals of London—Karan's parents.

Chapter 4

Rohit's deepest desire was for his family's contentment. The past year's chaos had left them feeling unmoored. He had never anticipated Rupali's betrayal, nor his own near-fall from grace, a lapse he deeply lamented. A fleeting affair was one thing, but not with someone who had been his wife's close friend for over twenty years. Yet, he couldn't deny the intoxicating allure of venturing into uncharted territory with Sakina. He paid close attention when Rupali spoke of Adil and Sakina's return.

The scent of musk, a fragrance that seemed to cling to Sakina like a second skin, drifted unbidden into Rohit's thoughts, a vivid reminder of her intoxicating presence. It was a scent that spoke of hidden depths, of a sensuality that both intrigued and unsettled him. He could almost feel the silken weight of her hair in his hands, that thick cascade of reddish-brown waves that tumbled down her back, framing her face like a fiery halo.

And her lips... He remembered the sultry pout, the way they curved into a knowing smile, hinting at secrets and desires. They were lips made for kissing, whispering intimacies, and drawing a man into her orbit. Sakina was, in every sense of the word, seductive. It wasn't just her physical beauty, though that was undeniable. It was the way she carried herself, the confidence in her eyes, the playful challenge in her voice. She exuded a raw, magnetic energy that left Rohit captivated and slightly breathless.

They had danced on the precipice of something more, a dangerous dance of stolen glances, lingering touches, and unspoken words. The air between them had crackled with a palpable tension, a forbidden attraction that had come dangerously close to igniting into a full-blown affair. The memory of those near-miss moments, the almost-kisses, the almost-confessions, still haunted him.

Now, Sakina was back. The news had sent a jolt of awareness through him, a mixture of anticipation and trepidation. The old feelings, his undeniable pull towards her, resurfaced with a force that surprised even him. He couldn't shake the image of her, the memory of her scent, the allure of her touch.

The question hung heavy in his mind, a persistent whisper that echoed his deepest desires: Would this time be different? Would the unspoken attraction finally find its release? Would they succumb to the magnetic pull that had always existed between them? The thought both thrilled and terrified him, a tantalising possibility that he couldn't quite dismiss.

Rohit had a deep aversion to unresolved stories and couldn't wait to meet Sakina again.

As Rupali happily gushed about the prospect of meeting Karan's family, Rohit was jolted back to the present and smiled indulgently at his wife. This was certainly positive news! Raagastar, his music management company, was currently flush with cash thanks to some very successful artist collaborations. They could afford to splurge on a fancy engagement and a grand wedding. Whatever Anisha wanted, he would ensure she got. After all, his daughter was a princess, and her wedding had to be the talk of the town.

The Jahangirs had been a name to reckon with in Dubai society for quite a few years, and he was going to make sure no one forgot that easily.

"Let's have a party, darling. It's time to celebrate. It's been so long since we all caught up, and hey … why don't you invite Adil and Sakina as well? It's the right thing to do if they're back in town."

"Err…are you sure Ro? Not sure they are really up to meeting big groups!"

Rupali had seen Rohit virtually ignore the Chaudhrys over the past year, when Adil had the cloud of a fraud investigation hanging over his head. They were pretty much social outcasts now after their return to Dubai.

She wondered why he was now suddenly eager to engage with them socially. In the past she would have believed it was because he was a genuinely empathetic and kind person who wanted to give his old friends a second chance. These days though, nothing fooled Rupali.

Rohit valued nothing as much as his own success. He was a cut-throat businessman who would stop at nothing to get what he wanted. Adil was now at the opposite end of the spectrum and far from the profile of the people Rohit wanted to have in his circle.

She wondered why her husband had suddenly decided to be nice to the Chaudhrys when he had barely contacted them since they left for London.

Was it Sakina and her everlasting allure? Rupali was no stranger to how men reacted to Sakina's sexy avatar. Voluptuous and irreverential to the core, she was impossibly forward, leaving nothing to the imagination, and they seemed to love it. Had she changed? she wondered.

None of them needed the drama Sakina usually brought to the party. Although she had seemed weak and defenceless every time Rupali had spoken to her during her stint in London, she hoped that Dubai would not bring back her former bitchy persona.

She would have to ask Anjali what to do.

For now, however, Rupali had a wedding to plan and nothing could mar her happiness at knowing that Anisha had finally found her perfect life partner.

Rohit was right, it was time they all got together again with their friends to announce this wonderful news.

Chapter 5

As Anjali drove home after meeting Sakina, her mind was swirling with thoughts.

Sakina had maintained herself amazingly well; there was no doubt about that. In fact, she appeared sophisticated and confident and ready to take on the world. Anjali was genuinely happy her friend had not let the past year's events leave a scar on her. And yet there was something shifty about Sakina's attitude she couldn't fathom. She was unwilling to discuss anything personal at all and was constantly guarded in her responses to Anjali, even though she was still probably the closest friend she had in Dubai.

Anjali missed her earlier persona – loud and hearty with a laugh that always showed her teeth and outfits that accentuated her voluptuous figure. " I'm massy not classy", she would say in good humour, knowing fully well how men reacted to her. She had been fearless of social opinion and did her own thing, unapologetically brazen at times.

And yet that had been the very quality that Anjali had always admired about her. That Sakina truly didn't give a hoot about what other people thought. She dressed to please herself and conducted her life in an erratic yet mesmerising way. Standing in the worst part of a crowded Deira market waiting to eat kebabs from a streetside vendor, just because she had read they were the most authentic in town. The very next day, she had gone up to the 85th floor of the Rush hotel at 6 am just to swim and take in the morning sunrise and the spectacular views at one of the highest rooftop pools in Dubai. Irreverential to the core, Sakina followed her own rules, and Anjali loved how fearless she had always been.

Now suddenly she was following the social norms of Dubai, playing nice and sophisticated and a girl who clearly wanted to impress.

"How boring", thought Anjali as she swerved to avoid a delivery rider cutting into her lane.

"You were everything that your husband was not, even if he was bankrolling you."

I hope your spirit hasn't died, my sweetheart. Don't let the circumstances take that from you."

As Anjali looked at her phone, she realised she had a missed call from Rupali and decided to call her back as soon as she was home. Hopefully Rupali would be chilled out about the fact that she hadn't been invited to lunch with Sakina.

Although Anjali had meant to figure out Sakina's game plan in Dubai, she was as much in the dark as before the meeting. Sakina was hiding something, and Anjali doubted it had anything to do with her husband's murky corporate affairs.

Chapter 6

Rupali was sitting in her favourite corner of the garden, making to do lists, when Anjali called. She hoped Anisha would have faith in her decisions regarding sartorial choices, venues for the functions, jewellery, and all the other wedding-related decisions that she had dreamt about for so long.

Her precious baby doll had finally found her prince charming. God had indeed been very kind to their family, she thought, shivering involuntarily at the memory of the past year and all the chaos that had unfolded. Despite Anisha telling her to take it slowly and allow Karan time to get to know their family over summer, Rupali's thoughts were rushing ahead like a freight train.

Rupali's dreams were a whirlwind of wedding preparations, a symphony of colour, music, and tradition. A kaleidoscope of vibrant silks and shimmering gold danced in her mind's eye. Her daughter, Anisha, was to be married, and every detail had to be perfect, a reflection of their family's love and blessings.

She envisioned the mandap, draped in marigold and jasmine, much like Rohit and her's had been all those years ago, its fragrant blossoms weaving a tapestry of auspiciousness. The air would be thick with the rhythmic chanting of the pandit, the sacred fire flickering, casting a warm glow on Anisha's radiant face. She pictured Anisha, a vision in a crimson lehenga with its intricate embroidery.

She dreamt of the elaborate decorations, the strings of fairy lights twinkling like a thousand stars, the floral arrangements overflowing with vibrant colours. She saw the faces of her family and friends, their eyes filled with happiness and blessings, their voices raised in joyful celebration.

Beyond the grandeur, her dreams held a deeper yearning. She wished Anisha happiness, a lifetime of love and companionship with her chosen partner. She prayed for a strong and loving bond between her daughter and her new family, a union blessed by generations of tradition and goodwill. She dreamt of Anisha's laughter echoing through a happy home, grandchildren playing at her feet, and a future filled with joy and prosperity.

Her dreams were a tapestry woven with love, tradition, and hope, a mother's heart overflowing with blessings for her beloved daughter. Each detail, each colour, each sound, was a prayer for Anisha's happiness, a testament to the enduring power of a mother's love.

The wedding would have to be perfect. She would ensure it was. Somehow, Rupali had convinced herself that her own marriage to Rohit depended on how well they fulfilled their only child's dreams.

All the best wedding planners and venues got booked up almost a year in advance. The children couldn't afford to dilly-dally with their decision. Summer was around the corner, and when they finally met Karan's family in London, she hoped they could drive some sense into the kids together and make arrangements for a brief Roka ceremony (a formal acknowledgement of the alliance), followed by an engagement party in Dubai and then of course a splendid wedding.

As she sat lost in her thoughts and plans for her daughter's perfect future, the phone rang and Rupali picked up on the first ring when she saw it was Anjali calling. She couldn't wait to tell Anjali her news. Anjali had known Anisha since she was three years old and would be thrilled to hear that Rohit & Rupali's baby girl would soon be settling down with the boy of her dreams.

"Babe …listen, thanks for calling back. I have the most amazing news!! Anju, you're not going to believe this"

As Rupali shared the happy news about Anisha's engagement plans, Anjali momentarily forgot her worry about Sakina.

Anjali and Rupali shared a profound bond, forged over two decades of close friendship in Dubai. Their lives were deeply interwoven, filled with shared milestones and joyous occasions. From establishing their first Dubai homes and helping each other navigate their new lives, to Anjali's first job, Sakina's driving test, Anisha's birth, Diwali celebrations at the Jahangirs', and Christmas gatherings, their shared experiences formed a vibrant and beautiful tapestry of memories, uniquely theirs, in the heart of Dubai.

"This is the most fabulous news, Rupali! I'm so excited for our princess."

Anjali was truly happy for Anisha. A lovely child, it had been heartbreaking to hear about all her problems with an obsessive past boyfriend who refused to take rejection lightly.

Hopefully, she would now have a brand new shot at happiness, and Anjali was thrilled for her.

"This is just the news I've been waiting for ...amazing. Happy to plan it all with you, sweetheart. Just tell me what you need "

"Well for starters Anju, Rohit wants me to organise this party at home sweetie. He's overjoyed of course and can't wait to share the news with all of you himself."

"How typical of Rohit", thought Anjali. Of course, this was one more triumph for the Jahangirs, and he would have to declare it publicly. Rohit and Rupali were known to throw the most lavish parties, sparing no expense with fantastic food, fun themes, music and entertainment. This would be no exception.

Rupali suddenly paused midstream in their conversation, remembering that she had wanted to ask Anjali about Adil and Sakina. In all her excitement, she had forgotten that they were planning to meet Sakina.

"Have you met her yet, sweetie? Should we set something up?"

Best to tell her the truth, thought Anjali. Rupali was completely trustworthy, and she knew she had been as concerned about Sakina's welfare as she herself had been. She didn't want Rupali to feel left out.

"Yes, I met her for a quick lunch on my own. Just wanted to see how she was doing, babe. Check what was going on with them ..."

As Rupali said nothing, listening carefully to Anjali, she continued.

" She looks amazing....a little overwhelmed at being back in town and not quite sure where their lives will take them, but I think she will be fine."

They were both shocked to learn that Adil and Sakina were now residing in an apartment bordering Sharjah, a far cry from their former glamorous life in a luxurious downtown Dubai high-rise with Burj Khalifa views. Neither of them ventured into that area during all their years in Dubai. It was clear the Chaudhrys sought anonymity, the reasons shrouded in mystery. Evidently, Adil Chaudhry's fortunes had taken a significant downturn.

"Did you speak to Adil?" Rupali asked hesitantly, referring to Sakina's husband. She knew the couple was very close to Anjali.

"I wish", said Anjali sadly. He won't speak to anybody. "We'll have to give them time, Rupali. Don't expect them to socialise the way they did when they were here earlier. Sakina needs to find her feet again, and we have to help her do that. No questions, no scrutiny into their lives until she confides in us herself—ok? Let's just try to help her stay afloat for a start."

Dubai's expat community was notoriously unforgiving, offering scant room for those seeking redemption. The city's relentless pace left behind those who had stumbled. With a constant stream of new, fascinating people, attention was perpetually diverted. A quick glance at social media showcased the dazzling social scene, the lavish gatherings, and the seemingly flawless lives that drew endless connections. Dubai didn't linger on setbacks; everyone was too consumed with ascending the social hierarchy.

Rupali felt a genuine wave of compassion for Sakina. Beneath the alluring exterior and playful charm, she was a kind soul who had once belonged and considered Dubai her home. Now, like the city's burgeoning, peripheral areas where they lived, Sakina and Adil were once again outsiders. Rupali understood the daunting challenge they faced in reclaiming their place.

Chapter 7

His voice, usually a low rumble, was now a harsh growl, each word laced with a raw, barely contained frustration. "You think you can just... walk away?" he spat, his voice burning into her ears. The air crackled with a tension that was both volatile and charged. Even through the phone, Sakina could feel him invading her personal space, his ominous presence a suffocating weight.

What the hell are you doing? Why didn't you pick up my phone, Sakina? Do you think I'm a bloody fool? Do you think I can't tell what's going on? You know what I want," he hissed, the words a dark promise. You know what you want, too. Don't play coy with me.

You are hooking up with that loser husband of yours again, aren't you? Do I have to remind you that I control every breath of his? Don't you ever forget that. "I'm not finished with you," he continued, his tone a low, dangerous whisper.

Sakina held her mobile phone to her flaming hot cheeks as she listened to this tirade.. Thank God she had got out of the lunch with Anju without her noticing something was amiss.

God—how would she ever understand what was truly going on? She had never been in a situation like this herself. Clever, super successful, glamorous go-getter Anjali was the editorial Chief of Dubai Glam, the UAE's foremost fashion publication. She was educated, independent, and powerful. Men would never dare speak to her like this.

Wiping a stray tear that had trickled down from the corner of her eye, Sakina tried to focus on what her nemesis was saying. God...how she hated him.

I'm in Dubai for the next two days, so make up some damn excuse and get to the Marriott, ASAP. I want to see you.

Sakina sometimes drifted into wistful reveries of her past life, a time when she had been a diva, adored by her husband and the object of every man's desire. Rohit, with his handsome, classy demeanour, had been no exception. She had always possessed a keen sense of when men noticed her; those were the days. Lazy mornings in satin sheets, breakfast in bed, and a life of limitless luxury: designer clothes, shoes, and her own fire-red Porsche, a birthday gift from her husband, emblazoned with a personal 'S'.

But the party had ended, and no one had prepared her for the harsh, unforgiving realities of the outside world.

"I'll be there," she murmured, hanging up the phone. A sense of resignation settled over her. The red satin negligee, delivered from London the previous week, now made chilling sense.

As she touched the silky fabric, a wave of revulsion washed over her. She imagined the words her friends would use to describe her. There was nothing romantic or sensuous about this arrangement. The weight of her current reality pressed down on her, suffocating her. She looked back at the woman she once was, eager to please, sexy and vibrant, with a cynical detachment. Now, no amount of concealer could hide the dark circles under the eyes. She stared at the stranger in the mirror, desperately trying to convince herself it was someone else living this life.

Adil could never know her secret. It would destroy him

She entered their cramped apartment to find her husband calmly sipping his tea, his expression a flicker of surprise at being caught idle. Sakina brushed off his reaction, launching into a cheerful recount of her day.

"Meeting Anju was wonderful, Jaan...I'm so glad we had lunch. It felt like I'd never left. The girls are thrilled to have me back. Anju's even insisting on hosting dinner next week so that we can catch up with Rupali and Rohit too."

Adil nodded silently, his face devoid of emotion, as she continued.

"Oh, and by the way, I'm off to a fashion photoshoot tomorrow and the day after, okay? Anju got me some free passes, and it sounds like a lot of fun. It's at the Marriott. She knows I love being around the models and seeing all the designer clothes. I might even get some professional headshots done if I have time. The photographers there are supposed to be top-notch."

Sakina looked at her husband, smiling indulgently at her, and thought about how easy it had become to lie to him. In fact, it became easier every single time she did. Did she have a lack of conscience, she wondered, or was it just that he no longer deserved a truthful partner who hung onto his every word and believed that he was the centre of the universe.

No – quite the contrary she thought silently furious as she looked at his stodgy frame and dirty glasses as he looked at her waiting for her to finish talking so he could go back to his Pakodas and Chai. There was no escape for her either way, she decided. Atleast not as of now.

Sakina Chaudhry would be back as Queen Bee in Dubai soon. She was sure of that. Whether with or without her husband would have to be decided in due course.

She left him to his tea and went off for a shower. The bathroom, barely large enough to turn around in, was a symphony of rust and neglect. A single, cracked tile on the floor was perpetually damp, a constant reminder of the leaky pipes that ran through the building's ageing infrastructure. She was sick of the mouldy, grout-laden tiles in the bathroom and the leaky faucet that the homeowner had promised to get fixed before they moved in and then never did.

At least the Marriott would have clean showers. She deserved some pampering.

Chapter 8

Anjali lived in the posh Jumeirah area of Dubai. With the glistening ocean bordering the bougainvillaea-laden villas and chic cafes, it was an area to see and be seen in. It didn't bother her that the area wasn't open to freehold buying yet and that she was still a tenant of Villa 23 on Al Wasl Road. Her stylish address had been home over the past 20 years of living in Dubai. There was absolutely no need to rock the boat now.

Anjali was extremely attractive. Her aura was a blend of cold, calculated elegance and raw, untamed power. She was a walking paradox, a vision of the future that had slipped through a crack in time. She did not merely wear avant-garde fashion; she *was* avant-garde fashion, a living, breathing testament to the power of radical self-expression.

She had cultivated her aura carefully in Dubai. No longer was she Anjali Sen, the struggling Junior Creative writer, desperate to get a break in mainstream publishing. Gawky and awkward she had barely known how to carry herself when she first arrived in Dubai. Her brilliant writing had often been overlooked given her underwhelming presence. It had taken her a long time to understand that perception was reality in Dubai and appearances mattered most. The more she was humiliated and ignored, the more she had silently vowed to fight back. Changing the definition of success, she had paid careful attention to the way she dressed and how she presented herself. Her garments, less fabric than constructed experience, were a symphony of textures: panels of iridescent silk clashed with matte and sculptural leather, while delicate, hand-blown glass shards seemed to float from the digital prints on some garments, suspended in a cage of blackened, articulated wire. Blacks, browns, greys, and taupe formed her unusual palette. The more she discovered fashion, the more she decided to shatter the existing norms and create her own playbook, on her own terms, at work and in life.

As she sat staring at the pile of books on her work desk at home, there was a sinking feeling in the pit of her stomach. Something was wrong with Sakina. She was sure of it. Although she had appeared cheerful and confident, there was also a distracted, vacant expression that was a million miles away. What could it be, Anjali wondered. How would they help her if she refused to tell anyone the truth about what was going on?

She would have to confront her demons at some point, and Anjali was willing to hold her hand through it—if only Sakina saw it that way.

Who would do the same for her? Anjali reflected. God knows she was struggling with enough ghosts of the past herself.

Forcing a positive outlook, she envisioned the upcoming celebration of Anisha's engagement, a grand affair hosted by Rohit and Rupali. The Jahangirs, she knew, would spare no expense.

As Simba, her golden Labrador, bounded into the study, she embraced him, receiving a wet, enthusiastic lick in return. "Yuck, Simba, what was that for?" Anjali laughed, rushing to wash her face before leashing him for their evening walk.

They took their usual route, a path leading directly to the beach behind her villa. Simba, as always, surged ahead, nearly tripping Anjali in his eagerness. The setting sun, bright and intense, momentarily blinded her as she stumbled forward, colliding with an evening jogger on the path.

"Oh my gosh, I'm so, so sorry!" Anjali exclaimed, attempting to untangle herself and Simba's leash from the stranger, feeling utterly clumsy.

"No worries …I'm perfectly fine," he replied cheerfully, helping her up and brushing off his clothes as Simba bounded back to her side. "Gorgeous," he said involuntarily, with a broad smile.

"Cheeky," Anjali retorted, smiling herself. He was handsome, in a charming, boy-next-door way. Life and its unexpected surprises! She rarely ran into anyone interesting on this path.

"Oops, I meant the dog. I'm sorry," said the handsome stranger, laughing at the misunderstanding. "I promise I don't usually ambush female walkers and their canines on this beach."

"I'm Anjali"

"I'm Abhay", he responded with a broad and disarming smile.

"If you're finished jogging, you can walk with me."

Even for her typically outgoing personality, Anjali was surprised by her own boldness and, worse, her desperation for company. She could almost hear her mother's warnings about talking to strangers. Yet, Abhay felt like an old friend, and they fell into easy conversation, strolling along the beach as if they'd known each other for years.

He told her that he had just moved to Dubai three months back and was in the process of settling down. Like Anjali, he had fallen in love with the Jumeirah area and decided to rent a beautiful apartment overlooking the ocean. It was perfect in every respect. A busy CEO in Tech, he kept long hours at work. "I need a space I can come home to and relax. The ocean on my doorstep is all I need to feel I'm home." He had moved to Dubai from his last assignment in Bangkok.

As they watched the sunset together, suddenly neither of them wanted the evening to end.

Abhay had never met anyone like Anjali before.

Her hair, a cascade of chrome-dipped tendrils, framed a face sculpted from ice and defiance. Her eyes, twin pools of molten brown, held a gaze that could dissect a soul with a single glance. Her lips, painted a shade of pale pink that seemed to absorb all light, were perpetually curled into a subtle, enigmatic smirk.

She wore her accessories like weapons: a neckpiece of metal that pulsed with a faint, inner light; rings that spanned multiple fingers, each tipped with miniature, razor-sharp obsidian blades; and shoes designed to defy gravity. Woman or warrior – he couldn't decide, but she was stunning in every way.

Anjali felt exactly the same. Abhay was attractive in an earthy way. He was 6 feet tall, with chestnut brown hair and light brown eyes. He appeared rugged and fragile in equal measure, which Anjali loved. Easy, friendly, and unassuming, he had an undeniable charm that she found quite irresistible.

As Simba tugged urgently at his leash, they hurriedly parted ways, agreeing to meet for coffee at the same spot over the weekend. She felt a surge of excitement that she hadn't felt in ages. Something about meeting Abhay felt so right.

Despite her professional success in Dubai and a huge circle of friends, Anjali was lonely. Something she was reluctant to admit, even to herself.

"See you very soon, Abhay," she said with an enigmatic smile as she walked away, knowing his gaze was following her into the orange–hued Dubai sunset.

It was a quarter past ten in the morning when Sakina Nawaz stepped out of her Uber ride and into the blinding sunshine as she made her way toward the Marriott hotel. She was a vision in her dusky pink dress, with her large Chanel sunglasses covering half her face.

She desperately hoped she would not run into anyone she knew in the hotel lobby. It was bad enough that she had lied to her husband. The last thing she needed was for someone else to pry into her affairs. Strategically avoiding the conference room where she knew her tormentor currently sat lording it over a board meeting, she picked up a key from the Bell Desk addressed to a fake name and escaped into the elevator. Luckily, the concierge was busy with morning arrivals and barely noted the glamorous lady who looked as if she had just misplaced her key card.

As Sakina entered the room on the 34th floor overlooking stunning views of the Arabian Sea, she caught her breath. The bedroom was a symphony of refined taste, with high-quality hardwoods, and sumptuous silk and its walls were adorned with expensive Artworks, carefully curated to create an atmosphere of sophistication. The entire atmosphere was one of tranquillity and opulent luxury, and as she opened the door to inspect the bathroom, she saw that it was a haven of indulgence in itself, with a deep soaking tub, a separate rain shower, and dual vanities. It was well stocked with luxury toiletries from renowned brands, soft bathrobes, and plush towels, enhancing the spa-like experience.

It had been a long time since she had been in a suite as luxurious as this one. Despite herself, her thoughts were flooded with the images of another time when her own high-rise apartment overlooking the Burj had looked like this.

Clutching the silk negligee in her hand, she sat on the bed and took a deep breath, quelling her sudden panic. This wasn't London, where she had lived as a virtual stranger, nor was it her plush home in Dubai, which she no longer lived in.

What was currently going on in her life was too crazy.. too dangerous. She was out of her depth.

An affair in an unknown city, far away from prying eyes was different. How on earth could he expect her to continue this dangerous liaison in Dubai.

She messaged her husband as a flush of guilt overtook her. "I'm here at the hotel in the shooting. Don't call me as the phone will be on silent. I'll call when the shoot is done".

There was no immediate response which usually meant that Adil was not online. Unlike Sakina, he was no longer constantly hooked to his phone or his WhatsApp messages. There was simply nothing urgent or pressing that he needed to take care of anymore. Life moved at a snail's pace for her husband these days, a far cry from his days in corporate life.

After having showered and changed, Sakina lay back against the satin sheets, switching on the TV mindlessly, watching a show as she snacked on the strawberries and chocolate she found in the room. She knew he would be up soon.

The sleepless nights in the gritty apartment had taken their toll, and she soon fell into a deep and dreamless sleep. She had no idea when Ali entered the room. He moved with a predatory grace, his footsteps muffled by the thick carpet, as he stood watching the figure comfortably reclining on his bed. She was a vision of beauty, her reddish-brown tresses cascading down her shoulders. "Darling," he purred, his voice a low growl that sent shivers down her spine." It's so good to see you "

She immediately woke up and tried to rise, her heart pounding in her chest, but he waved a dismissive hand. "Stay put," he commanded, his voice laced with a dangerous edge.

He approached her slowly, his eyes never leaving hers. "I've been thinking," he said, his voice dropping to a conspiratorial whisper, as he traced the outline of her face with a stubby finger. "…. that our relationship needs to be formalised."

Her breath hitched in her throat. She knew what he was about to say, but she couldn't believe it. Ali smelt of stale cigar and whisky and a combination of body odour and bad breath that was utterly revolting. His eyes bulging out of his grotesque, swarthy face made him look even more unpleasant than she remembered.

"I want you to marry me," he declared, his voice firm and unwavering.

Her eyes widened in disbelief and shock. She had never expected this. She had always considered him a dangerous man who played powerful games, but never the kind who would settle down.

His eyes gleamed, reflecting the shock he'd etched onto her face. A cruel smile twisted his lips. "Don't feign surprise," he rasped, his voice laced with biting sarcasm. "This isn't a request. It's an order."

She tried to speak, her jaw working, but terror had seized her tongue. No sound escaped her lips. She was paralysed.

He leaned in, his breath a hot, oppressive wave against her skin. "You belong to me now," he growled, his voice a low, predatory rumble. "And I won't relinquish my claim."

Ali Rez was a man accustomed to absolute control. He had been Adil's mentor and benefactor at ABQ, a pivotal figure in mitigating the fallout after the scandal that had forced Adil's abrupt departure.

As the bank chairman, he commanded immense power, skillfully managing the damaging publicity that had all but destroyed her husband's career. "It's a temporary measure," he assured them upon their arrival in London. Public attention is fleeting. We simply need to weather the storm until the markets recover. There's too much at stake right now. Remain inconspicuous until I give you further instructions."

Sakina had harboured doubts about Ali's altruism, but Adil was convinced his mentor had his back.. "Ali will always be there for us, Sakina. He's our lifeline," he had insisted.

Despite Ali's polished demeanour, Sakina had detected an underlying menace.

One desolate London evening, while her husband was away, she received the call that irrevocably altered her relationship with her husband's boss.

There was always a price to be paid for freedom.. Ali's ultimatum was stark: he would ensure that Adil was convicted, condemning him to a lengthy prison sentence, unless she complied with his demands. After all, he had complete control over the investigation into the fraud at ABQ bank.

Trapped, with no recourse, she had been forced to agree.

Now, she stared into his eyes, her own mirroring her fear and desperation. She understood the futility of resistance.

"Yes," she whispered, her voice a fragile, broken sound.

A triumphant smile spread across his face. "Good girl," he purred, his voice laced with a chilling satisfaction.

He pushed her back on the bed, his weight crushing her and his legs pinning her down, even as his grip was still tightening around her wrist. Her heart pounded in her chest, and her mind was racing with fear.

She knew she had made a terrible mistake, but it was too late now. She was trapped, a prisoner of her own fear and the ruthless man who held her captive.

Chapter 9

"Did you see the invite from the Jahangirs babe?"

Manish and Naina sat in their dining room, savouring the Baked Alaska their new chef had just presented. It was absolutely delicious.

Manish and Rohit were business partners and the success of Raagastar, their music management company had been a huge triumph for both the men.

As far as Manish was concerned, it was all he needed to be validated by Naina's father.

After all, he was the man with the mega bucks who had invested in his son-in-law's business venture.

"So, the Jahangirs are finally having another party after ages. It must be a very special occasion", smirked his wife Naina.

Rupali and Rohit had been unusually quiet over the past six months, and there was a huge buzz about their troubled marriage.

"Serve that arrogant bitch right", thought Naina to herself. She envied Rupali, mostly for her close-knit friendships with her girlfriends. God, the way they had all stuck together through thick and thin the previous year had been nauseating to watch.

Naina herself had very few friends, although her parties were always well attended and were the talk of the town.

Yet, she was consumed by loneliness after the lights and the music had died down. Manish was perpetually buried in his work, and she knew that it had become a great excuse for him to spend time away from home whenever he got a chance. It was infuriating that he, too, thought the world of Rupali, as if she were some unblemished goddess who always walked the straight and narrow—an icon of beauty and grace.

Manish looked at his wife, who sat silently staring down at her dessert.

"A penny for your thoughts, darling?"

Naina was a vision of delicate beauty. She was a petite Indian woman whose sharp features—a finely sculpted nose and piercing light green eyes—hinted at a willfulness that belied her small frame. Every inch of her was adorned with the trappings of unimaginable wealth.

A cascade of diamonds, each the size of a dewdrop, glittered at her throat, part of an intricate necklace that looked like woven starlight. Matching earrings, heavy with more of the precious stones, framed her face, catching the light with every imperious turn of her head.

Her designer wear, a vibrant yellow silk kaftan that flowed around her like liquid sunshine, whispered of haute couture and limitless budgets. Even the delicate Tory Burch slippers on her feet were customised and embellished with tiny, sparkling gems. There was an air of practiced nonchalance to her every gesture, a subtle arrogance that spoke volumes about a life lived in the lap of luxury.

Naina's throaty, hoarse laugh, a sound as distinctive as her diamond bracelets, echoed as she dismissed the value of some unseen object. "My thoughts …worth that much? Please." She flicked a manicured hand. "The Jahangir's invite? Of course, let's go. Perfect excuse to wear my new Dior dress." The vibrant red silk, she mused, would make her emerald eyes blaze, especially paired with those newly acquired Blahniks.

Spoilt rotten was an understatement. Shopping, mail-order catalogues, and globe-trotting without her husband defined her everyday life. Her childhood, marked by her mother's death, had been a parade of material gifts from her tycoon father, a substitute for the affection she craved. The unspoken pain, the isolation, remained buried. There was no point in voicing it.

She had played the part her father had scripted for her, forcing herself to appear as a dumb brunette who knew nothing of corporate affairs. Nobody cared about her educational background or her keen business acumen. She knew that Manish hated her pampered princess avatar, and sometimes, she exaggerated it just to watch him squirm. After all, his own background was entirely different.

Manish leaned over to give her a perfunctory kiss on her forehead. A daily ritual that was a hollow gesture. Their marriage, devoid of intimacy for months now, felt like a polite charade. He played the role of a responsible friend, oblivious or indifferent to the chasm between them.

She envied Rupali's friendships, the easy companionship, the shared laughter, and the unconditional acceptance. A longing for genuine connection, for a soul to confide in, gnawed at her. Someone, anyone, who could offer the warmth she desperately needed and didn't get from her own husband.

She knew what her father would say if she spoke to him about it. " Don't like him…leave." He had no time or inclination to involve himself too deeply in his daughter's life.

Unfortunately, Naina had nowhere to go and no way to get Manish to leave.

Chapter 10

In a glorious, leafy suburb of the opulent Emirates Hills, the Jahangir Villa was buzzing with activity. Rupali had meticulously curated their guest list with Anjali and Rohit's input. Very few people had not been invited from Dubai social circles. Of course, Anisha and Karan were not in town yet, but it was still the perfect opportunity to celebrate the big news of their impending engagement with their friends.

"Isn't it a bit early for all this, Ro?" she had asked her husband tenuously, despite his enthusiasm. After all that they had been through the previous year, Rupali was still overcome with hesitation. "We haven't even properly met Karan's family yet."

A wave of protectiveness washed over her, a fierce maternal instinct that mingled with a deep-seated fear.

She knew there would be whispers, the hushed conversations that followed her daughter's every move, the envious glances, the veiled compliments that carried a hidden sting. Rupali fully believed in the effects of the *Nazar*, the evil eye, a superstition deeply ingrained in their culture, a belief that malicious intent could bring harm and misfortune.

For years now, Rupali had ensured she tied a black bracelet with little black beads around Anisha's wrist, the amulets worn for protection.

After the stalking nightmare Anisha had gone through in the US, Rupali had taken no chances and done it all, every ritual, every precaution, to shield her daughter from the unseen forces that threatened her happiness.

But the worry lingered, a persistent shadow that clung to her heart. She prayed fervently, seeking divine intervention, a shield of protection, a blessing that would ward off the evil eye and ensure her daughter's happiness.

What if something horrible happened to Anisha again?

Rohit, though, was unconcerned. " Don't be silly. Try and stay positive, darling. It's important to celebrate these occasions properly and publicly!"

As far as he was concerned, there was no sane reason any young man would not want to marry into their family. After all, they were the Jahangirs, with an impressive fortune to boot, and Anisha was his only daughter, as brilliant as she was beautiful. There was absolutely nothing that could go wrong, and he would ensure that.

Rupali was quiet. Anisha had specifically requested that she curb Rohit's attempts to make a big deal of his daughter's engagement. Flamboyance was second nature to her father, and she knew it. " Mom, please tell him not to go overboard with the celebrations just yet, okay? Of course, Karan and I are certain we want to be together, but I definitely am not ready to share this with the whole of Dubai just now."

Rupali knew that her daughter resented the Dubai gossip circles. Some aunty or the other who was whispering about what had gone wrong and why a boy had stalked Anisha in such a nightmarish way. Despite the wave of public sympathy, she was aware of what they were saying.

"She's a little too extroverted, no? Wearing all these micro minis and going out to the clubs in Boston. What did she expect, *haan?*"

These girls are all over the place these days, smoking and substances and God knows what not. Money is unlimited, no.. that's the tough part. Rupali and Rohit have completely spoilt their princess. "

Basically, Anisha knew that her privilege constantly made her a huge target both within Dubai and away from home. No matter how hard she worked or how much she had achieved independently, she was always seen as her parents' pampered princess, and she was sick of it.

She was always defensive about her family's wealth and had embraced a minimalistic lifestyle of late in New York.

"I'm fine just to have around 50 close friends and get married at a private ceremony, Ma," she had said.

However, even she knew that her father had very different plans. Nothing was private anymore in Rohit Jahangir's universe. It was just a well-orchestrated dance in the social melee that was Dubai. There was no escaping that. The Jahangirs were too well known.

"Don't worry about it, darling. I'll make sure we're only doing things the way Karan and you want them, okay?"

Anisha had agreed, knowing fully well that her father would do exactly what he thought was befitting of his status. She was used to that!

Rupali busied herself with the invitations to the big soiree to announce their daughter's betrothal. As she called Anjali first to invite her, her best friend had some good news of her own to share.

"Babe, I want you to meet someone who may become important in my life, ok? His name is Abhay."

She tried her best to sound nonchalant even as Rupali squealed in delight...Whaaaat???!!!

"Anju, that's amazing. Why are you mentioning it to me only now? God, I'm dying to know the details. Who is he, and when did you meet him?"

"Ha ha ha … let's not go overboard here. It's just been a few months, but hey.. I like him, so let's see".

Anjali was careful not to sound overenthusiastic about Abhay. Rupali had a tendency to over romanticise this. This was a good "situationship", she shared now with Abhay and she was really glad they had met. The rest …well she would need to figure that out.

Rupali had been dying to know the details. Anjali had been single for so long now, and despite all her friends' attempts to set her up with eligible men, she had always held on fiercely to her independence.

"Relationships cause needless complications yaar. I'm better off single, she had laughed."

This sounded different, though, thought Rupali as she listened to Anjali. Who was this stranger who had swept Anjali off her feet? There was only one way to find out.

"Listen, Anju, bring Abhay to the party on Saturday night," she said. It will be fun, and no one needs to know more than you're willing to let on, babe.

It's a big group anyway. It'll be fun to meet him, and we can just say he's an acquaintance from out of town visiting you."

It sounded harmless enough to Anjali. It had been nearly 3 months since she had initially stumbled into Abhay at the beach, and she herself was surprised at how fast things had moved since then.

Anjali, a whirlwind of sharp wit and sharper stilettos, juggled deadlines and hemlines with the same effortless grace. As a fashion editor, her life was a curated chaos of runway shows, frantic fittings, and the ever-present hum of the city.

Abhay was a symphony of easy charm and quiet strength. Their meeting was created by a clumsy tangle of limbs and startled apologies, but the connection had been instant, a spark ignited between them.

They discovered a shared love for vintage films, a mutual disdain for pretentious art, and a surprising affinity for obscure jazz records as their meetings continued. Anjali, used to the fleeting, superficial interactions of her world, found herself drawn to Abhay's genuine curiosity and thoughtful observations.

Their dates were refreshingly simple: home-cooked meals, prepared with laughter and shared stories, sprawling conversations that stretched late into the night. Anjali, who'd always preferred the sleek anonymity of restaurants, found a surprising comfort in the warmth of Abhay's kitchen. He'd effortlessly whip up aromatic Thai curries with freshly ground pastes, while she, a surprisingly adept baker, would produce decadent desserts.

Their evenings were a tapestry of shared jokes, whispered secrets, and the comfortable silence that spoke volumes. They discussed their dreams, their fears, their pasts, each revelation drawing them closer. Abhay, a global nomad and a techie, saw the world through a different lens, capturing the beauty in the mundane, a perspective that captivated Anjali, whose world often revolved around the manufactured perfection of fashion.

As their connection deepened, their conversations grew more intimate, exploring the nuances of their desires and vulnerabilities. The physical attraction that had simmered from their first encounter blossomed into a tender intimacy, a slow dance of exploration and discovery. Their evenings, once filled with casual banter, now held a quiet smouldering intensity, a shared understanding that transcended words. They found solace and passion in each other's arms, their connection deepening with every shared glance and whispered touch. Anjali, the fiercely independent warrior, had discovered a warmth and tenderness she never knew she craved, and Abhay, the quiet observer, found a vibrant, passionate soul who mirrored his own.

Life was suddenly perfect for both of them.

Chapter 11

The air hummed with hushed conversation and the delicate clinking of crystal. A long, polished mahogany table stretched across the room, its surface gleaming under the soft glow of a magnificent chandelier. Each place setting was a work of art: delicate china edged in gold, gleaming silverware, and crystal glasses that sparkled like captured starlight.

In the centre, a breathtaking floral arrangement, a riot of orchids, roses, and lilies in pastel hues, cascaded from a silver epergne. The room itself was a vision of elegance, with silk-draped walls and plush velvet seating, with the lighting casting a warm, inviting glow. Soft music played in the background, adding to the refined ambience. Every detail, from the impeccable service to the exquisite cuisine, spoke of opulence and refined taste.

Rupali stood in the midst of the room, looking absolutely radiant in a peach silk evening gown with tiny seed pearls embroidered all over. Her hair was set in loosely flowing waves, the way she knew Rohit liked it.

He was deep in conversation with the Russian Ambassador and his wife, who had been delighted to accept their invitation. The Jahangirs were, after all, known to be incredible hosts. Rohit, in a navy blue dinner jacket, grey trousers and a crisp white linen shirt bearing the monogram R. J. on his cuffs, looked as handsome and distinguished as ever.

The guest list was a combination of Dubai's who's who. People from the diplomatic circles mingled with business tycoons. There were celebrities from the music world and fashionistas, whom Rupali barely recognised, but Rohit had insisted that they invite.

Once the perfunctory conversations were in progress with all their guests, Rupali, a vision in her peach shimmery gown, moved through the throng of Dubai's elite with the practiced grace of a seasoned hostess, checking that the starter courses were all going well and that champagne and Chardonnay were in full flow.. Her smile was radiant, her voice a melodious chime echoing the upper echelons of the city's social strata.

Yet, beneath the meticulously crafted veneer of warmth and charm, a hollow ache resonated within her. The air buzzed with the clinking of champagne flutes and the murmur of hushed conversations. But to Rupali, it all felt distant, a stage play where she was forced to perform a role she no longer understood.

This opulent gathering, ostensibly to announce their daughter, Anisha's, engagement, felt less like a celebration and more like a strategic manoeuvre. Why had her husband, Rohit, insisted on this grand, impersonal affair? Why these specific guests, a carefully curated blend of business associates and diplomatic figures? Anisha's happiness, in the midst of this ostentatious display of opulence, seemed completely inconsequential.

Rupali watched as Rohit, wearing his mask of effortless charm, held court with a group of men whose laughter sounded harsh and ruthless. She knew the language of these gatherings: subtle power plays, veiled negotiations, and the silent exchange of favours. But tonight, the game felt particularly cold.

She remembered the intimate, joyous gatherings of their early years, when celebrations were marked by close friends, laughter and shared meals, not by the calculated display of wealth. Now, even Anisha's engagement, a moment that should have been steeped in familial warmth, was being presented as a strategic alliance.

Rupali's heart ached for her daughter, for the innocence that was being subtly sacrificed on the altar of ambition. Would Karan be able to meet Rohit's expectations?

Rupali felt a growing sense of detachment as she moved through the room, offering polite smiles and engaging in polite conversation. The carefully orchestrated movements of the evening, the practiced smiles, the calculated pronouncements, all felt like a performance, a charade that left her feeling empty and alone. She wondered if anyone else felt the same dissonance, the gap between the glittering facade and the hollow core. She felt the weight of unspoken questions, the silent yearning for something real, something genuine, amid all the artifice.

She couldn't wait for her own friends to arrive, and thankfully, it wasn't too long before they did.

Anjali and Abhay made a wonderful couple as they walked in confidently. Despite being a newcomer to Dubai, Abhay was a highly successful Tech tycoon, which in itself was enough for him to hold his own in a sea of strangers. An easy conversationalist with great business acumen and an even bigger sense of humour, he was an instant hit with the guests, regaling them with anecdotes from his scuba diving adventures in Thailand and his many misadventures since he landed in Dubai.

"He's really quite a guy", said Rohit to Anjali as they stood watching Abhay surrounded by a group of guests hanging onto his every word. He couldn't decide whether he liked him or was just the slightest bit envious of his unassuming charisma that everyone seemed to adore.

"That he certainly is", said Anjali, feeling secretly proud that Abhay had even managed to impress the suave Rohit Jahangir, who was used to being the life of the party himself.

"You lucked out, Rupali said, observing Abhay too. What a charmer he was!

"And of course he did, too, "…she quickly added, turning to smile at her attractive friend as Abhay blew Anjali a flying kiss and winked from his corner of the room.

Chapter 12

The Chaudhrys were back.

Sakina walked into the party fashionably late in a royal blue evening dress and a sparkling tiara arranged on her massive updo. Two coppery ringlets framed her sensuous face, and as usual, she felt the cynosure of all eyes. Adil followed her hesitantly, lagging a few steps behind. He had begged to excuse himself from the party, which Sakina had firmly declined.

Rohit & Rupali's party, a beacon of their former social standing, was a daunting first step. Sakina had clung to the hope that her friendship with Rupali would offer a sliver of solace, a lifeline in this sea of disdain. It was time they made their first public appearance.

But as they entered the party, the warmth she'd anticipated turned into a chilling wave of silence.

The clinking of champagne flutes faltered, the murmur of conversations ceased, replaced by a tense, electric stillness. Sakina could feel the weight of a hundred pairs of eyes, dissecting their presence, whispering judgements that hung heavy in the air.

"Look who's back," a sharp, venomous voice said through the silence.

"The Chaudhrys," another voice echoed, a mix of shock and morbid curiosity.

"Shit...after all that he did. That's crazy"

" I didn't even realise they were still together!"

Sakina's heart pounded against her ribs, a frantic drumbeat against the silence. She could see the shock etched on faces she once considered friendly, the thinly veiled disgust in the eyes of those who had once fawned over them. Like venomous snakes, the hushed whispers slithered through the room, each syllable a cruel reminder of their disgrace.

Adil, usually so confident, so commanding, stood beside her, a shadow of his former self. His silence was more painful than any accusation, a testament to the magnitude of their fall. He seemed to shrink under the weight of their scrutiny, his gaze fixed on the intricate patterns of the Persian rug beneath their feet.

Sakina felt a surge of desperate anger and fierce protectiveness towards her husband. She wanted to scream, to defend themselves, to demand their respect. But the words caught in her throat, choked by an overwhelming sense of shame and humiliation.

Rupali, her face a mask of carefully constructed composure, approached them. Her smile strained, her eyes filled with a mixture of pity and apprehension. "Sakina, Adil," she said, her voice barely audible above the rising murmur of the crowd. It's… good to see you."

Sakina knew it was a lie, a thin veil over the unspoken truth. Rupali was embarrassed by the reaction of their friends. They were pariahs, unwelcome guests in a world that had once been their own. The opulent ballroom in her friend's villa now felt like a stage for their public humiliation. The whispers continued, a relentless chorus of judgement, echoing the fear that gnawed at Sakina's soul: would they ever be accepted again?

"Thanks, darling. It's so good to see you," she said softly as Rupali quickly hurried off toward her other guests.

As beads of perspiration suddenly made their way down the back of her dress and a glass of Prosecco was thrust into Sakina's hand by an overzealous waiter, her knees went weak as she noticed who was walking over toward them.

"Adil, my man. It's so great to see you finally. I've been asking Rupali to ask you guys over for the longest time. How are you? When are we grabbing a game of Padel? I've missed my tennis buddy." Rohit sounded boisterous and cheerful and Adil felt grateful for his warmth and affection. After all they were such old friends. He needed Rohit's great contacts now more than ever if he had any chance of finding another job.

"Thanks Ro, he blurted. You are in great shape as usual my friend. You guys have reversed the ageing process."

"Hello sweetie", said Rohit smoothly turning to greet Sakina with a practiced ease that sent a shiver down Sakina's spine as he casually draped his hand across the small of her back. The gesture, seemingly innocuous to the watching crowd, was a starkly different language to Sakina. It was a familiar touch, a ghost of a past she'd tried to bury, a reminder of the almost–affair that had sizzled between them.

The years melted away, and her raw, undeniable attraction for him surged back, a tidal wave threatening to drown her carefully constructed composure. Seeing him again, amidst the glittering chaos of the party, ignited a dangerous spark, a forbidden desire she'd thought was long extinguished.

Desperate to mask the turmoil within, Sakina began to consume the champagne with a frantic urgency, the bubbles a poor substitute for the emotions she was trying to suppress. The alcohol, instead of calming her nerves, fuelled her recklessness, emboldening her to act on impulses she knew she should restrain.

She found herself drawn to Rohit throughout the evening, her laughter too loud, her eyes too bright as she followed him around like an adoring puppy dog joining the entourage who were hanging onto his every word. She leaned into him, her voice a husky whisper, her words laced with a dangerous flirtation that was unmistakable. Her behaviour, once elegant and refined, devolved into something brazen and inappropriate.

Rupali watched with growing horror as Sakina wouldn't stop downing the alcohol. She couldn't reconcile the woman before her with the Sakina she thought she knew. "Since when...?" she murmured, her voice laced with disbelief, "Since when did Sakina become... this?"

Adil, his face a mask of mortified silence, tried to intervene, although his attempts to reign in his wife's escalating behaviour were futile. He was a broken man, stripped of his former authority, and his words carried no weight. He could only watch, speechless, as his wife's disgrace unfolded before the entire Dubai elite.

Anjali, her usually warm eyes narrowed with anger, watched Sakina's descent with a mixture of disgust and disappointment. "When will she ever learn?" she muttered, her voice tight with frustration. Sakina was behaving like an absolute fool.

Sakina, oblivious to the growing censure of her friends, continued her reckless pursuit of Rohit, her inhibitions dissolving with each sip of champagne. Then suddenly the unthinkable happened as she stumbled over a fold in the Persian carpet and fell flat, throwing her arms up to shield her face instinctively. As her overly tight blue dress immediately ripped, a flash of garish underwear was exposed to the stunned onlookers. A collective gasp rippled through the room, the sound of social ruin.

The snide remarks began, whispers turning into open mockery, the air thick with judgement.

"Wardrobe malfunction ha ha ... Of course, we should have guessed the dress is from Dragon Mart, not Dior."

"Gosh, what a completely insane character she is "

"Sakina needs help and desperately ...why the hell did Rupali invite her. I mean it's not like anyone missed her!"

"Look at Rohit ...he's literally salivating over her. Poor Rupali "

"Didn't they have an affair last year? They were caught somewhere together, no?"

Sensing the impending storm, Rohit immediately distanced himself, his face a mask of polite detachment. He became a casual observer, another face in the crowd, leaving Sakina to face the consequences of her actions alone.

Rupali, her face etched with a mixture of pity and disgust, quickly gestured to a waitress who offered Sakina a wrap to cover herself. She was furious.

"Take them home," she instructed her chauffeur firmly, her voice cold and clipped as the Chaudhrys, their return a catastrophic failure, were escorted out, much to the disappointment of the curious onlookers. Their disgrace complete.

Rupali ignored the scathing looks of her guests, her eyes desperately seeking Anjali, who was the only person who could help her process what had just happened.

Meanwhile, her husband was already back in the midst of his cronies, asking for a mike.

"My friends…this party is for you… for us. it's a celebration…a celebration, he slurred. My princess is getting married. Rupali and I will host you on a Mediterranean cruise for Anisha's engagement. Karan …my son-in-law-to-be is from London…a huge, absolutely huge business family. Been there for ages. The kids are in New York now, but you will…we will meet them soon. We will all meet soon".

Rupali's face bore a frozen smile as she clutched Rohit's arm, willing him to shut up. He was drunk out of his mind. She herself was still trembling with the debacle of Sakina's behaviour, but the show had to go on.

Grabbing Rohit's mike, she said in a tense voice, "It's honestly wonderful to have you all here with us. What a great celebration of friends like family. We look forward to the summer and having the formal engagement party with all of you attending. Thank you for all the love and blessings for our children. Please enjoy yourselves and have a wonderful time!"

As Rupali looked desperately across the room at her abruptly ending her speech, Anjali picked up the cue and asked the DJ to start playing *"Dilli walli girlfriend"*, a Bollywood hit on full blast. As the lights dimmed and the music blared, the crowd moved onto the dance floor, heaving their bodies and swaying to the rhythm. It was one more happy night to party, and the post-mortem on the drama caused by the Chaudhrys could wait!

Chapter 13

Naina's perfectly manicured nails tapped a staccato rhythm on her champagne flute, her eyes gleaming with undisguised satisfaction. The Chaudhrys' spectacular implosion at Rupali's party was a delicious spectacle, a vindication of her carefully cultivated disdain. "Such classless, cheap people," she murmured, a thin smile on her lips. Sakina's drunken display, the ripped dress, the tawdry underwear – it was a public humiliation of epic proportions.

She couldn't fathom how Rohit tolerated Rupali and her circle of "friends." *They* were beneath him. *She*, Naina, was his equal. She possessed the looks, the poise, the social standing, and, most importantly, the immense wealth of her father, a man whose influence stretched across Dubai's financial landscape. Rohit Jahangir, a man of such undeniable charisma and raw magnetism, deserved better than Rupali. He deserved her.

Naina was trapped in a loveless marriage, a gilded cage built on convenience and social obligation. She yearned for the kind of passion, the raw, unbridled heat, that she imagined Rohit possessed. The thought of his hands on her, his lips on hers, sent a forbidden thrill through her veins.

However, Rohit was wary of Naina's lineage. Kamal Gupta was known to be a ruthless man. He found Naina's icy perfection intimidating, her carefully constructed facade impenetrable. He preferred the fiery, unrestrained energy of women like Sakina. Despite all her failings, at least she was real.

Naina was used to biding her time to get what she wanted in life. Patience, she knew, was a virtue. Her father, the silent power behind Raagastar, had unwittingly laid the groundwork for her plan. Rohit soon had no choice but to notice her as a significant stakeholder. Her father was now old and blinded to the treachery unfolding beneath her very nose. But she knew exactly what Manish was up to.

Naina was sick of being the hapless victim of betrayal. It was time to plot her own agenda, one that would shatter these men's carefully constructed world and reveal a truth far more shocking than they could ever have imagined.

As Abhay and Anjali left the party, they sat silently in the car. There was just too much for Anjali to tell him. How would he ever understand?

He allowed her to stay lost in her thoughts. He had really enjoyed the party and meeting Rohit and Rupali, whom he knew were Anjali's close friends. Unfortunately, the arrival of the Chaudhry couple had caused an enormous scene. Despite her deplorable behaviour, Abhay felt really sorry for Sakina. Anjali had told him that they had to leave Dubai the previous year in ignominy after an alleged financial fraud in Adil's bank. She had also made a passing reference to their good friend Dipika, who had died under mysterious circumstances, but refused to discuss any of these happenings in greater detail.

Abhay was still treading on delicate ground in their relationship. Despite being very attracted to Anjali and quite serious about investing in their current relationship, he did not want to pry into her friends' lives until she herself was comfortable sharing the details. He could sense an invisible wall between them tonight and was unsure how to react under the circumstances.

Anjali's expression was grim. After all, it was she who had insisted to Rupali that Sakina's earlier avatar as a nymphomaniac was now water under the bridge. She had reassured her that their friend had changed. Worst of all, Anjali was mortified by how Rohit had been flirting overtly with Sakina. Utterly deplorable behaviour!

As Abhay watched Anjali in the backseat of their Lexus, he could see a tear on her cheek and quickly grasped her hand.

"Anjali…babe, are you ok?"

"I worry for you, sweetheart. I know these girls are your friends, but you need to draw the line somewhere. You are so involved with them and getting needlessly drawn into their controversies. "

"Rupali and Rohit are lovely people individually but there is zero chemistry between them. Am I the only one to see how far they have drifted apart?

And Sakina is a good person suffering from the weight of scandal and embarrassment. She deserves your compassion, babe – not your anger."

Anjali looked at Abhay, not really hearing his words. What did he know? How could he possibly ever understand all that they had been through together the previous year?

"I don't recall asking you for your opinion on my friends Abhay", she said in a bitchy tone that took him aback. She had never spoken to him this way. He was seeing a different side of Anjali.

Anjali was immediately contrite. The poor guy had no part to play in this drama.

"Hey, it's really late and I'm super tired. I hope you don't mind me not wanting to discuss any of this right now and with you!"

They travelled the rest of the ride home in stone-cold silence – Abhay was inwardly fuming, but for now, he would let it be. There was nothing left to say.

Literally slamming the door in his face, Anjali abruptly stormed off toward her villa. He could see how upset she was. Obviously, she wasn't going to get into details with him. She had known these friends for over 20 years in Dubai. They were more like family to her.

Abhay drove home silently. He couldn't help feeling that there was much more to all of them than met the eye, and he wasn't sure it was worth the trouble to discover their secrets.

Chapter 14

Sakina woke up bleary-eyed in their miserable apartment to find Adil missing.

Looking at her phone, she realised she had several missed calls from Anjali. "Shit…something had happened but what? Why was she blanking out? She remembering tripping on that damn carpet but nothing beyond that from the previous night."

Adil had obviously helped her to get home and then got her into bed. "But where was he now?" she wondered.

Rohit's handsome face, his deep voice and his arm around her was what she did remember. Oh God…had she misbehaved? Was that why Anjali was calling her so furiously? Was Rupali mad at her? This was supposed to be their great comeback to Dubai society. After all no one but Rupali would even invite them to any such party anymore. Had she botched it up, she struggled to remember but her head hurt. "Where the hell was her husband Adil?"

Adil had escaped very early in the morning to his long time retreat in Dubai – Perks, a café he had visited several times in the past. He desperately needed to clear his head.

Perks sat squarely on the crossroads of Al Quoz, a tangible link to Dubai's fascinating metamorphosis. The surrounding streets, once echoing with the clang and clatter of industry, now pulsed with a different kind of energy – the creative hum of galleries, design studios, and independent ventures. The very asphalt beneath Adil's feet bore witness to the city's remarkable evolution, a journey from a sun-baked, dusty outpost to the glittering metropolis that now stretched towards the horizon.

Perks itself was an institution, a steadfast presence amidst the shifting sands of progress. Run by a kindly old Emirati gentleman whose name everyone knew but few formally used, it predated the area's artistic renaissance. The café was the lifeblood of the industrial workers and nascent office crowd in its early days. They would arrive in droves, their mornings and evenings punctuated by the ritual of a crisp sambousek – the savoury spinach encased in delicate filo pastry – and the soul-warming embrace of steaming hot Karak chai.

The aroma of cardamom and ginger, the signature scent of Perks, was a constant in the neighbourhood's olfactory landscape. With his gentle smile and encyclopedic knowledge of local lore, the old Emirati owner Abu Hamza had been the first to introduce the now-ubiquitous Karak chai to this corner of Dubai. It was a simple offering, but it became a cornerstone of the community, a shared comfort that transcended backgrounds and professions. Perks had been there as the first skyscrapers pierced the skyline, the desert bloomed with manicured gardens, and the once-quiet roads swelled with the relentless flow of modern life. It was a silent observer, a repository of countless stories whispered over steaming cups, a comforting constant in a rapidly changing world.

Adil sought refuge in the familiar embrace of Perks this morning, not for their famed Karak chai, but for their signature Arabic coffee. It was a brew unlike any other in the city, a robust and potent concoction, deeply roasted and subtly spiced with cardamom. He hoped its strong, earthy notes would cut through the fog that had clung to his mind since the unsettling encounter the previous night.

As he stepped inside, the familiar scent of roasted beans and a hint of cardamom was a comforting balm. It truly felt like coming home. The old Emirati owner, perched behind the counter, offered a silent nod of recognition. Adil settled into his usual booth, the worn leather familiar beneath his fingertips.

The Arabic coffee arrived in a traditional dallah, accompanied by small, handleless cups and a plate of dates. He poured himself a small measure, the dark, viscous liquid promising a jolt of clarity. The first sip was intense, a welcome bitterness that spread through his senses, followed by the warm, aromatic whisper of cardamom. He savoured it slowly, letting the rich flavour coat his palate, hoping it would indeed sharpen his dulled thoughts and bring some semblance of order to the chaos in his head

The familiar aroma of roasted beans did little to soothe the turmoil churning within him. Dubai's relentless sun beat down outside, starkly contrasting the gloom that had settled over him since the previous night's disastrous party.

Sakina. The very thought of her sent a fresh wave of bitter disappointment crashing over him. Her behaviour… slutty was the only word that kept echoing in his mind, harsh and unforgiving. How could she have been so oblivious? Didn't she see him teetering on the edge? He needed the support of people like Rohit and Manish Gupta, their professional networks his only lifeline to claw his way back. And there she was, a whirlwind of inappropriate laughter and wandering hands.

He swirled the lukewarm coffee in his cup, the dark liquid mirroring the bleakness of his thoughts. This version of Sakina was a stranger. A lush, he thought with a distaste he couldn't suppress, drowning her sorrows in alcohol and seeking fleeting attention. Their second chance, the fragile hope they had nurtured, was crumbling before his eyes. They were undoubtedly doomed in Dubai if she didn't pull herself together. Yet again.

Lost in this vortex of despair, Adil barely registered the young woman who had just walked into the café and then suddenly he took notice. Something about her gait, a certain familiarity in her posture, tugged at a distant memory. He squinted, his vision blurred without his glasses, which he had forgotten in the car. A baseball cap shadowed most of her face, offering only a fleeting glimpse. He dismissed the feeling of déjà vu, attributing it to his frayed nerves.

But as she turned to leave, he got a fleeting glimpse of her face and a sharp intake of breath caught in his throat. He did a double-take, his heart hammering against his ribs. The profile... it was undeniably her. But how? The impossibility of it slammed into him with brutal force. She was gone. They had mourned her.

A cold dread seeped into his bones. Was this it? Had the stress finally pushed him over the edge? Were the antidepressants playing tricks on his mind, conjuring ghosts from the past? He felt a wave of nausea rise within him. The cheerful chatter of the café, the clinking of cups, and the general hum of life around him suddenly felt alien and distorted.

He pushed himself up, the chair scraping against the tiled floor. His legs felt unsteady, his mind a chaotic confusion and fear. He stumbled towards the exit, the image of her profile seared into his vision. He couldn't make sense of any of it. He needed to talk to someone, someone who could ground him in reality. Anjali. He had to call Anjali.

As he got back into his car he saw frantic missed calls from his wife. Despite his annoyance, he messaged her back. "Had an early morning meeting in Al Quoz. I thought you would sleep in today? Will be back soon."

Suddenly, within the fraction of a second, Sakina was not his primary cause for concern.

He decided to make a stop on the Jumeirah beach road before he went home, but not before he had made another call.

Chapter 15

Anjali groaned, the remnants of the previous night's revelry pounding a relentless rhythm against her temples. Unwelcome and harsh sunlight streamed through the gap in the curtains, exacerbating her throbbing headache. As fragments of the party began to coalesce in her foggy memory, a fresh wave of anxiety washed over her. Rupali. What on earth was she going to say to Rupali?

Anjali knew with a sinking feeling that the blame lay squarely at her own feet. She was the one who had so enthusiastically pushed Rupali to include the Chaudhrys in their grand soiree. It seemed glaringly obvious now why Rohit had been so happy to extend the invitation. His rampant flirting with Sakina replayed in Anjali's mind, each suggestive glance and lingering touch a fresh stab of embarrassment. He deserved to be called out for his boorish behaviour, no doubt. But then again, Sakina hadn't exactly been a picture of resistance, had she? Anjali sighed. Of course, the waiter's incessant champagne refills hadn't helped, but Sakina always seemed to find a way to court drama. "Why did she have to do this every single time?!"

A wave of longing for the recent past washed over Anjali. Life had been much simpler and more serene when the Chaudhrys were tucked away during their London exile. They were back in Dubai, bringing their messy entanglements and public displays.

A difficult conversation with Rupali loomed large. This kind of behaviour was simply unacceptable within their circle. Anjali hoped Rupali would also have a stern word with Rohit, but she held little optimism. Rohit Jahangir was a creature of habit, a flamboyant and unapologetic womaniser who operated under the assumption that his charm could conquer all. Everyone saw it, everyone whispered about it, except perhaps his adoring wife, who seemed perpetually blind to his indiscretions. Anjali braced herself for the inevitable fallout, knowing the delicate balance of their friendships had been irrevocably disrupted.

She deeply regretted snapping at Abhay the previous night. The poor guy had done absolutely nothing wrong. In fact, she was so grateful for his calm and reassuring presence – a complete contrast to the chaos around her.

Anjali's phone rang, interrupting her inner dilemma, and she was surprised to see who the caller was.

Naina Gupta!

Anjali …it's me Naina. Listen, I'm so sorry but I really thought you could use a sounding board today, and I just wanted to reach out. I know I'm not in your inner circle. You girls have known each other for so long. But sometimes it helps to just share things with someone unbiased and with no vested interest. I honestly just want to help, to listen to you in complete confidence and without any judgement. Sakina is dealing with a lot right now. I don't think she deserves to be subjected to this scrutiny and meanness. I'm actually feeling so bad for her. I really want to support her in any way that's possible.

Naina knew she had Anjali's attention.

Having carefully assessed Anjali for many years now, she saw in her a woman who deserved her respect and admiration. They had met socially many a time, but never got beyond pleasantries for whatever reason. But Naina knew Anjali saw her for who she truly was and not just as Manish's wife or her father's daughter. To the outside world, she was the epitome of a pampered princess, the only daughter of real estate magnate Kamal Gupta, showered with every imaginable luxury. But beneath the veneer of privilege lay a sharp intellect and formidable business acumen, honed by an MBA from Bocconi in Milan.

Her father, however, had never recognised the steel beneath the silk. In his patriarchal world, a daughter's role was decorative, not decisive. He had swiftly arranged her marriage to the awkward and perpetually insecure Manish, installing his son-in-law as the head of their sprawling business empire and investments. It was a decision that had ignited a quiet fury within Naina, a silent scream against the limitations imposed upon her. In her eyes, Manish would always be more of her father's pliable employee than a true husband, a dynamic she suspected her father had engineered precisely to maintain control over them both.

For all his outward affection, Kamal Gupta subtly resented his daughter's intelligence, dismissing her insights with a condescending wave of his hand. "Stick to your travels and your passion for fashion design, Naina," he'd often say with a dismissive chuckle.

Naina reminded him of her docile mother and brought back memories of a time he would rather forget. He couldn't ever imagine that his daughter harboured ambitions far beyond fabric swatches and exotic locales. Despite

Naina's impressive educational credentials, pursuing an undergraduate degree in business from Warwick in the UK, followed by her MBA from Bocconi, Milan, she was still not taken seriously by her father. She hankered for his love and approval all her life, yearning for a greater role in the family business.

Naina had always been an astute observer, though, and she had noted the subtle shifts within Anjali's established circle of friends, the palpable tension simmering beneath the surface in the wake of Sakina's recent antics. Once a seemingly impenetrable fortress of camaraderie, the original group now appeared fractured, vulnerable. This, Naina realised with a keen sense of opportunity, was her moment to gain acceptance.

Anjali, a woman of undeniable strength and sharp professional instincts, was exactly the kind of ally Naina needed. She recognised a kindred spirit, a woman whom superficialities wouldn't sway. Building a genuine connection with Anjali could be the key to navigating the complex social landscape and, perhaps more importantly, finally asserting her capabilities beyond the confines of her father's expectations. The time for observation was over. It was time to act, to bridge the distance and forge a connection with the woman who could become her most valuable confidante. If there's one thing Naina had learned from her father, it was that connections mattered most of all. She finally had a chance to get through to Anjali!

Naina's sensitivity truly touched Anjali.

Thanks so much for calling Naina – that's so kind of you to think about Adil & Sakina and what they're going through. Most people who were at the party last night are probably striking them off their contact lists forever. But they think of Dubai as home, and the only reason they are back is to resurrect their lives here in Dubai.

Honestly, I'm not sure how human we are if we cannot give people a second chance."

Naina listened to her carefully as Anjali seemed grateful for her considerate and compassionate attitude. It was the longest they had ever spoken.

The friendships forged within Dubai's expat society, Naina mused, were often as ephemeral as the desert mirages that shimmered on the horizon. Out of sight, quite literally, meant out of mind. Beyond the meticulously planned Ladies' Nights, the lavish Friday brunches, the glamorous race days, and the endless round of social obligations, a genuine personal connection was a rare commodity. It was a somewhat melancholic truth, reflecting on the often superficial nature of the bonds they formed. Wealth and the outward trappings of social influence held a disproportionate weight, often overshadowing the deeper nuances of individual personalities.

Yet, in that moment, as Naina listened intently to Anjali's raw outpouring about the previous night, she felt a connection that transcended the usual fleeting interactions. Anjali, clearly shaken and deeply troubled by Sakina's behaviour and Rohit's audacity, was in need of genuine comfort, and Naina offered it freely, without reservation. She didn't hold back her empathy or understanding, recognising the genuine distress in Anjali's voice and the vulnerability in her eyes.

As they discussed the messy fallout of the party, a different kind of bond began to form. It wasn't based on shared social calendars or the need to maintain a certain image, but on a shared understanding of the complexities of relationships and a moment of shared vulnerability.

Naina felt that reaching out to Anjali had been the right thing to do, a step beyond the superficiality that often defined their interactions and towards something potentially more meaningful. She had made a new friend and had a proper conversation, after a very long time.

Chapter 16

When Anjali finally disconnected the call, she was feeling much better. It had been good to unburden herself to someone like Naina who wasn't as embroiled in this whole saga as they all were. She tried to reach Rupali, only to find that her phone was unreachable, as was Sakina's. Anjali knew she would need to give them time before having the difficult conversation that needed to be had.

She had tried calling Abhay too, but got his voicemail that he was in an urgent work meeting and would call back. Anjali had called in sick herself.. She often worked from home and went to her client meetings and shoots directly. Her team was now accustomed to not seeing her in office regularly.

She looked down at Simba, who was looking at her soulfully as if to remind her that she had still not taken him for a walk.

"Let's go, baby boy," she said, stretching her long limbs and getting up to take him out.

Anticipating a message from her office, Anjali was quick to grab her phone, as it beeped angrily on her kitchen counter.

Her thumb hovered over her phone screen, about to open the group chat, when a new message popped up, arresting her movement. It was a personal message, not a group notification. The sender's name displayed starkly: Dipika.

A shiver, cold and sharp as an ice pick, went through Anjali. Dipika. Dead for over a year. Murdered. They had all attended the funeral, the raw grief of Dipika's family still echoing in her mind. There was only one Dipika still saved in the contacts on her phone because she couldn't bring herself to delete the number.

Her breath hitched. *No, this can't be. There has to be some mistake.*

Hesitantly, she opened the message.

The screen illuminated her face, casting an eerie glow in the dim room. The message was simple, almost banal, but its very existence twisted it into something horrifying: "Anjali, are you there?"

No context. No explanation. Just those four words, radiating an unnatural chill.

Anjali's heart hammered against her ribs, a frantic bird trapped in a cage. Her fingers trembled as she scrolled up to check the number. It was Dipika's. She had always had a black circle as her profile pic – "it's different na?" she'd joke. The exact number Anjali had saved years ago, the number they had used to share jokes, plan outings, and confide in each other.

A wave of nausea washed over her. Her mind raced, searching for any logical explanation. A cruel prank? A mistake in transferring numbers? But the rational part of her brain was losing ground to a primal, instinctive dread.

The room seemed to grow colder, the silence amplifying the frantic thumping of her heart. Anjali stared at the screen, the four words burning into her consciousness. It was as if the message had opened a door, a crack in the world, and something... *other* was peering through.

A sense of profound unease settled over her, heavy and suffocating. It wasn't just shock or disbelief. It was a bone-deep horror, the kind that whispers of things that defy explanation, things that violate the natural order—the horror of a message from the dead.

She gripped the kitchen counter, willing herself not to pass out as she saw who it was from and read the message further.

"Guess what, darling? I'm back.

I know about your little arrangement. You thought you were clever, na?"

You underestimated me. You mistook my trust for weakness, my kindness for stupidity. A big mistake. The money you so cleverly snatched? It belongs to me. Every single dirham.

Now, it's your turn to pay."

This wasn't a random message. This was *Dipika*.

Anjali gasped as the room began to spin around her. This couldn't be happening. Dipika was gone. They had mourned her collectively and put her murderer behind bars.

What kind of a sick joke was this now? Somebody was messing with her mind.

Only one person would know what to do.

Chapter 17

Adil had almost reached Anjali's residence when he suddenly tripped over an uneven surface on the pavement and fell heavily to the ground with a loud thud as his head hit the curb. He felt a searing pain in the back of his head as if he had been branded with a hot iron, and the world seemed to tilt on its axis, as his head swam, and then he mercifully blacked out.

A passerby, seeing him fall, immediately rushed to his side, dialling 911 on his phone as Adil lay slumped on the ground, unconscious. The ambulance arriving within minutes with paramedics quickly assessed Adil's condition, realising the severity of his head injury and potential blunt force trauma.. They quickly rushed him to Medwell hospital, sirens wailing, their lights flashing through the traffic.

At the hospital, Adil was quickly rushed into the emergency department, where a team of specialists worked to stabilise his condition and quickly rush him into the critical section to perform a CT scan. The nursing staff, following protocol, contacted the next of kin listed on Adil's phone's ICE contacts - Sakina Nawaz.

Sakina had been at home making some lunch when she received the call. She was desperately going over the events of the night before as she waited for her husband to return home. She would speak to Adil first and then apologise to the rest of them.

As she listened frantically, the voice on the other end calmly explained that her husband had had an accident and was admitted to the Intensive Care Unit of a leading hospital. She needed to get there as soon as possible.

Terrified, Sakina immediately ordered herself an Uber ride with trembling fingers and rushed to the hospital, her heart pounding in her chest." Adil had to be alright. How... how would she ever survive without him?"

Thankfully, Medwell hospital was not more than a 15-minute ride away, although to Sakina it felt like an endless journey as her head was swirling with dark thoughts.

En route, she called Anjali as well, urging her to get to the hospital as soon as she could.

Coming back to Dubai had been a mistake. Poor Adil was so incredibly stressed; maybe that caused him to pass out like that. Sakina tried to stop the thoughts racing through her brain. " What the hell had happened to Adil?"

As soon as she arrived at the Medwell hospital, she rushed to the duty doctor at the Intensive Care Unit.

"What happened? Where is my husband? Oh my God – is he alright? Why isn't anyone telling me anything?"

"Stay calm, ma'am. We are doing the best we can. Please wait here until we know more. Your friend Ms. Anjali Sen is already here."

In the ICU, Adil lay unconscious, his body fighting for life. The doctors worked tirelessly, their faces etched with concern, but Adil's condition remained critical. Sakina, her face pale with worry, was directed to the ICU waiting room, where she saw Anjali waiting, calm and reassuring as always, as she hugged Sakina and told her it would all be ok.

Soon, Rupali had arrived as well, and both of Sakina's dearest friends were right there by her side, as she knew they would be. No questions asked – the three of them sat there with their hands clasped tightly, praying for Adil's recovery.

Anjali's mind was swirling with thoughts, but now was not the time to tell the girls anything about the message she had received.

They need to focus on Adil's survival first.

The hours passed, each one an eternity for Sakina. Finally, the doctor emerged from the ICU, his expression grave. "The results of the CT scan are not very good, I'm afraid. The scan has revealed a crescent-shaped area of high density, the specific location and shape of which is characteristic of a subdural hematoma. The size of the hematoma and any signs of pressure it might be exerting on the brain tissue will still need to be assessed".

After the three women listened in shock to the diagnosis, Anjali went after the doctor to ask if they would immediately communicate these critical findings to the emergency physician or the neurosurgeon on call. The report had clearly indicated that there was a major blood clot pressing on Adil's brain, the result of a severe head injury.

Adil's condition was critical

Sakina's heart sank. She knew the gravity of the situation, but she clung to hope, praying that Adil would pull through. Remembering that they may need financial help, she sent Ali Rez a terse message.

"Adil is in the hospital …looks like a bad head injury. I'm here with him. There's no one else. Could you please transfer some money?"

Ali responded instantly.

"Will take care of it – some of our guys can come to help you with it. Just tell me what you need"

"The creep had a heart", thought Sakina, grateful that he wasn't planning to come to the hospital himself and intrude on her privacy. That would have been unbearable.

Poor, poor Adil!

Desperate and miserable, Sakina mustered up every ounce of strength and prayed. She would change herself. She would stop blaming him for all the shit they had been through last year. The poor guy must have been under enormous stress.

"Was he at home when it happened, sweetie?" asked Anjali gently, as they sat together at the hospital.

"No, actually, he had apparently collapsed on the street in Jumeirah … around a block away from your house" Sakina had been puzzled when the hospital's admissions team had informed her of this. What had Adil been doing that early in the morning in Jumeirah? He certainly hadn't mentioned any meetings to her.

The doctor walked in at that very moment to update her. "I'm afraid your husband will have to undergo neurosurgery. We're doing everything possible to stabilise vitals before he undergoes surgery. There's no telling if the damage is transient or permanent. We'll just have to wait and see. But for now – he isn't responding or showing any signs of consciousness at all. Let's hope for the best but prepare for the worst."

Flanked by Anjali and Rupali, both of whom were now waiting with her in the ICU waiting room at the hospital, Sakina looked frail and very frightened.

"We're there with you, sweetheart," Rupali whispered as she squeezed her hand.

Thank you…she said, a single tear falling down her cheek. She had never felt more afraid or alone.

As Adil lay in the ICU awaiting the neurosurgeon's arrival, Anjali insisted that Sakina go and get something to eat. The poor girl looked like she was about to faint. Rupali quickly led her away toward the cafeteria to get a cup of coffee.

As Anjali quietly entered the ICU to check what was going on inside, she could see Adil lying there hooked up to an IV. The silence of the room was only broken by a series of hoarse, guttural sounds emanating from Adil. They were harsh, animal-like grunts that sent a jolt of fear through Anjali. For hours now, he had been lying there motionless and semi-conscious, a victim of his circumstances.

As Anjali watched him, his fingers suddenly began to twitch rhythmically, and his head moved slightly from side to side, as if he were struggling to escape a terrible dream. Then, his eyes suddenly fluttered open, unfocused and clouded. A strangled whisper escaped his lips, a name that hung heavy in the sterile air.

"I saw her……. she's back."

"Who is back? whispered Anjali, completely shocked. She couldn't believe what her ears were hearing.

"Dipika…she's back".

When Anjali called her to give her the news about Adil's fall, Rupali had been truly shocked. They were just about getting over the debacle of the previous night.

Her hand flew to her mouth, her breath catching in her throat. Rohit was standing right in front of her, about to leave for work.

"Rohit," she whispered as she hung up the phone, her voice trembling, "Adil… he's had a bad fall and has a very bad head injury." The words felt foreign, heavy with disbelief. Adil, always such a solid guy, so full of life, collapsing like this? It was unthinkable.

She looked at her husband, expecting to see a similar shock reflected in his eyes. Instead, Rohit continued to scroll through his phone, his expression impassive. "Hmm," he murmured, barely looking up.

Rupali's disbelief morphed into a sharp sting of anger. "Rohit, did you hear me? Adil had a horrible fall and now has a blood clot in the brain! It's serious!"

He finally glanced up, a dismissive wave of his hand accompanying his words. "Well, I'm sorry to hear that, but what do you expect? The man drank like a fish. Bound to catch up with him eventually."

Rupali's blood ran cold. The hypocrisy was staggering. "Are you even listening to yourself?" she hissed, her voice low and dangerous. " It was an accident, Rohit! You're blaming Adil's drinking? Have you completely forgotten your own behaviour last night at our party? You were practically falling over!"

Rohit's eyes narrowed. "That's different. It was a party."

"Different?" Rupali's voice rose. "Adil is fighting for his life, and all you can think about is justifying your own excessive drinking? Sakina needs us, Rohit. Her husband, her rock, is in the hospital. Don't you even bloody care?"

A wave of protectiveness for her friend washed over Rupali. Sakina would be devastated, terrified. She needed her friends around her, a strong support system to lean on. Without a second thought, Rupali reached for her phone and dialled Anisha's number.

"Anisha, beta," she said, her voice tight with emotion, "I have some difficult news. Adil Uncle… he's had a bad accident and a severe head injury."

There was a sharp intake of breath on the other end. "Oh, Mumma! That's awful. How is Sakina aunty?"

"She's… she's trying to be strong. Listen, sweetheart, I know we were hoping to come and see you soon for the meeting with Karan's parents, but with everything happening here…"

Anisha's voice was immediately understanding. "Don't even worry about it, Mumma. Adil Uncle's health is what matters right now. Summer is ages away. We can always reschedule." Rupali felt a wave of relief wash over her. Her daughter's empathy was a balm to her frayed nerves.

As she hung up, Rohit's voice cut through the air, laced with resentment. "Why do you have to get so involved with those Chaudhrys? It's not your responsibility. You have your duties here. Surely they have enough doctors and nurses to look after him."

Rupali turned on him, her eyes blazing. "Enough doctors and nurses? This is about 20 years of friendship, Rohit! Sakina needs support, and I will be there for her, just like Anjali is" He watched her storm off in cold fury. True to her word, Rupali ignored Rohit's bitter pronouncements. Her focus was entirely on Sakina.

At the hospital, post-surgery, Adil lapsed into a coma. There was nothing more they could do from a medical standpoint but wait and hope he would come out of it. The doctors had already informed Sakina that it was quite likely that there had been some brain damage.

Rupali took charge of the situation. She organised everything from arranging for food and drinks to coordinating with the hospital staff, ensuring Sakina didn't have to deal with the logistical nightmares. Anjali, on the other hand, provided a constant stream of emotional support. She sat beside Sakina, holding her hand, offering words of comfort, and simply being present. There was no question of mentioning what Adil had said to her, but it was deeply distressing for Anjali. Now was not the time, though, for anything but to pray for Adil's recovery and take care of Sakina, she told herself.

Their actions weren't born out of obligation, but from a deep, genuine love and concern for their friend.

There were no long, drawn-out conversations about Sakina's struggles, no intrusive questions about Adil's condition or how he fell. Just a silent, unwavering presence that spoke volumes. They understood that in times of crisis, sometimes what a person needs most is not words but the reassurance of knowing they are not alone.

And then, without a word or a question, Naina Gupta joined their small but determined group. She simply arrived at the hospital with a huge fruit basket, her eyes filled with concern, ready to do whatever was needed.

Arriving at the hospital Naina observed the scene with a sense of awe. In the often superficial world of Dubai's social circles, where relationships seemed to be built on appearances and fleeting connections, the bond between Rupali, Anjali, and Sakina was a stark contrast. She had often found herself entangled in the shallowness of this world, caught up in the endless cycle of brunches, shopping trips, and gossip sessions. But here, witnessing these three women's quiet strength and solidarity, she felt a pang of longing for something more real in her own life.

The way Rupali and Anjali instinctively knew what Sakina needed, the way they anticipated her every need without being asked, the way they created a safe and supportive space around her – it was a powerful reminder of the true meaning of friendship. It was a bond forged not in the fires of shared social events or mutual acquaintances but in the crucible of shared experiences and genuine care.

As the hours ticked by, Naina was drawn to their quiet strength. She realised that true connection wasn't about exchanging pleasantries or attending the right parties, but about being there for someone in their darkest hour, offering a lifeline of support and love. Inspired by their example, Naina made a silent vow to cultivate deeper, more meaningful relationships in her own life, to move beyond the superficiality that had so often defined her interactions.

Together, the three women formed a protective shield around Sakina, offering practical help, a listening ear, and unwavering emotional support. They knew the road ahead would be long and uncertain, but they were determined to stand by their friend until Adil was back on his feet. Their solidarity was a silent testament to the enduring power of friendship in the face of adversity.

During the long nights at the hospital, Sakina's thoughts often drifted to Rohit. He hadn't even bothered to call or visit Adil after his surgery. He was as aloof as ever and refused to engage with her life. Was this all she meant to him? Despite everything that had transpired over the past few years, Adil had been a loyal friend to Rohit. And yet, Rohit was punishing both of them for some inexplicable reason, and Sakina had no idea why. He could be ruthless and self-serving when it suited him. Although Adil was unconscious and didn't realise what was going on, Sakina fully felt the weight of Rohit's rejection. There was no longer room for them in his busy and successful life. Rohit Jahangir had no time for losers. Looking at her husband, frail and dependent as he lay on the hospital bed battling for his life, Sakina deeply regretted the choices she had made in the past. Adil was a decent man. He didn't deserve to suffer like this. She would make it up to Adil... if he survived. Oh God, she prayed, please let my husband survive.

Rohit's aloofness and resentment faded into the background, irrelevant in the face of the genuine care and concern his wife Rupali demonstrated. Her loyalty lay firmly with Sakina and the quiet strength of their unwavering bond. Sakina felt deeply grateful for that.

Chapter 18

The news of Pamela Chaudhry's impending arrival in Dubai from New York rippled through the already tense situation in the Chaudhry family. Adil's cousin, Pam, was moving for her job as the head of a major logistics conglomerate, a significant transfer that thrilled her. Rupali couldn't help but think the timing was cruelly ironic. Sakina was barely holding herself together, and now a new dynamic was about to enter their lives.

When Pam called Sakina, her voice was warm and immediately sympathetic. "Sakina, my darling, I was so shocked to hear about Adil. I'm on my way to Dubai now. Don't you worry about a thing. I'll be there to help you in any way I can. Adil is my cousin, my brother, you know that."

Still reeling from the shock and constant worry, Sakina was too emotionally drained to process much. Anjali, ever the pragmatic one, gently advised her, "Sakina, you should let Pam help. Any support right now will be a blessing."

When Pam's flight landed, it was Anjali who offered to pick her up from the airport. As Pam emerged from the arrivals gate, Anjali was genuinely taken aback. She was strikingly beautiful, almost like a fashion model who had stepped off a runway. Her trendy layered hairstyle framed a face adorned with golden-brown tinted hair. Her features were perfectly sculpted – a refined aquiline nose, captivating light brown eyes, and exquisitely shaped lips. Her flawless complexion prompted a fleeting thought in Anjali's mind about possible cosmetic enhancements. How could anyone look so effortlessly stunning at thirty-five?

It quickly became apparent that Pam's beauty was matched by her sharp intellect and decisive nature. She seamlessly transitioned into her demanding new role, but her influence didn't stop there. Gradually, almost imperceptibly, she began to weave herself into the fabric of Adil and Sakina's lives. Still fragile and overwhelmed, Sakina found herself unable to resist Pam's well-intentioned but increasingly dominant presence.

The doctors remained cautious about Adil's recovery. He was out of the Intensive Care Unit and moved to a special ward, but his progress was slow and uncertain. The waiting stretched into days, each one heavy with unspoken anxieties.

One quiet evening, Anjali sat in Adil's hospital room, her laptop open but her attention drifting. Sakina had finally agreed to go home for a few hours to rest, urged by Rupali and Naina.

Anjali's heart ached seeing the dark circles under Sakina's eyes, a testament to the endless nights spent in vigil at Adil's bedside. Rupali, equally concerned, gently steered Sakina towards the hospital exit. "Go home, Sakina," she urged softly, her voice laced with compassion. "Let Anjali stay with Adil tonight. You need to rest, even if just for a few hours."

Sakina resisted, her gaze fixed on the closed door of Adil's room. The doctor's words echoed in her mind, each syllable a hammer blow: *interrupted blood supply...potential brain damage...be patient...pray for a miracle.* Her world had tilted on its axis. Finally, on the cusp of professional success, Adil lay still and unresponsive. The chilling prospect of him being a paraplegic haunted her waking hours, painting a bleak and uncertain future.

Anjali placed a comforting hand on Sakina's arm. "We're here for you, Sakina—both of us. Please, let me stay. You need to gather your strength." Finally, exhaustion etched on her face, Sakina nodded, a silent plea for good news in her tear-filled eyes.

The sterile silence of Adil's room pressed down on Anjali. The white and blue walls felt cold, contrasting to the warmth she wished she could offer. The array of life-saving equipment – the rhythmic blips of the ECG monitor, the whoosh of the advanced airway devices, the steady drip of intravenous medication, and the ominous-looking suction machine – hummed a constant, unsettling tune. It was a room suspended between hope and despair.

Anjali settled into a corner, her laptop open, a feeble attempt to distract herself. But the sterile environment and Adil's stillness triggered a wave of unwelcome memories. Dipika's face flashed in her mind, followed by the grim procession of her funeral, the hollow rituals that offered no solace.

A dark thought slithered into Anjali's consciousness: *Adil is as good as dead.* She immediately recoiled from the negativity, yet the seed of fear had been planted. It intertwined with another, more insidious worry – the feeling that someone was actively trying to smear her reputation, to cast doubt on her loyalty to Dipika.

A nasty little voice in her head sneered, "Loyal friend? Don't make me laugh! You took 'helping' Dipika to a whole new level, didn't you? You helped yourself quite nicely, too." Anjali squeezed her eyes shut, trying to silence the venomous whispers.

She looked across at Adil, a strong, dependable man now lying utterly vulnerable. In the past, even without Sakina knowing, she had confided in him, finding a steady ear and sound advice. A desperate longing for his consciousness washed over her. She needed him to wake up, hear what was happening, and offer his quiet strength.

Fear was an unfamiliar guest in Anjali's heart, but now it had taken root, a cold knot of anxiety tightening in her chest. The uncertainty surrounding Adil, coupled with the unsettling feeling of being targeted, created a suffocating sense of dread.

Chapter 19

The chic waterfront bar of the Dubai Harbour glittered with the reflection of yachts and city lights, a stark contrast to the darkness brewing within the shadowy figure seated alone at a secluded corner table. The clinking of ice in her whisky on the rocks was the only sound that punctuated the intensity of her thoughts.

She hated this fake, pretentious city that had destroyed her: the glitz, the glamour, the lies.

"Close friends," she sneered silently, her gaze fixed on the shimmering water. "What a pathetic charade." Rupali, Anjali, Naina – a carefully constructed facade of camaraderie. Each one of them, she mused, was a master of disguise, their smiles and sympathetic words nothing more than elaborate masks. Beneath the surface of their polished exteriors lay a network of secrets, dangerous and volatile, waiting to be exposed.

A slow, predatory smile touched her lips. Their past, that carefully buried history they thought was safely locked away, was about to resurface. And where else but in the glittering, unsuspecting city of Dubai? How naive they had been to believe their actions would remain hidden, that no one would ever unearth the truth of what they had done.

Her thoughts lingered on Rupali—the "ice maiden," as she privately called her. Always impeccably dressed, radiating an air of cool sophistication that belied whatever darkness lurked beneath. And her husband, Rohit Jahangir, the seemingly charming and successful business tycoon. What secrets did their gilded cage hold?

Then there was Anjali, the epitome of control and intellect, her professional life a testament to her meticulous planning. Yet, beneath that composed exterior, the shadowy figure sensed a fragility, a carefully guarded vulnerability. Anjali believed she held all the reins, but soon, she would discover just how wrong she was.

And Naina Gupta, the newcomer. Spoilt little rich girl and Daddy's pampered princess. A curious addition to their little clique. What was her story? What were her motivations for aligning herself with Rupali Anjali and Sakina? Was she a genuine friend, or was she playing her own game, seeking some unknown advantage? Naina was a stranger who had suddenly got very close to the girls. She'd have to dig deeper and find out more about her, too.

The ice in her glass had almost melted. With a decisive movement, she picked up her phone. Her fingers danced across the screen, finding the familiar number. She held the phone to her ear, the anticipation building with each ring.

"Hi" Her voice was low, a husky whisper that held a chilling undercurrent. "I'm getting closer to the truth. Don't worry. I'm still here… in Dubai. And I'm not leaving until I make these bitches pay." The line went silent, but the promise hung heavy in the air, a vow whispered into the Dubai night, carrying the weight of long-simmering revenge.

Chapter 20

The disquiet had been gnawing at Anjali for days. The single, cryptic WhatsApp message had sown a seed of unease, and Adil's delirious words had allowed it to sprout into full-blown anxiety. Despite the lack of further messages, the initial shock lingered. The memory of Dipika's tragic death the previous year, a public spectacle that had gripped Dubai, was still vivid. The investigation, the closure, the perpetrator behind bars – it all seemed so final. Could this message truly be a cruel prank, timed to coincide with Sakina's return and Adil's vulnerability? It felt disturbingly targeted.

Anjali had subtly probed Rupali and Sakina, but both of them were shocked and put it down to a nasty prank. After all, anything was possible with technology these days. Neither of them had received anything similar. Anjali remained convinced that she was the sole recipient of this unsettling communication. The urge to question Adil directly was strong, but the doctors' stern warnings about avoiding any stress for him, coupled with Sakina's fiercely protective vigilance, made it impossible. Sakina hovered around Adil like a guardian, her grief and worry manifesting as a barrier to anyone who tried to engage him in any meaningful conversation.

The Chaudhrys move to a more comfortable apartment, facilitated by Pam's efficient organising, was a small relief in an otherwise tense atmosphere.

Finally, feeling the weight of her secret becoming unbearable, Anjali decided to confide in Abhay. The glow of the Dubai Marina lights painted streaks across the window as they sat at an outdoor bar on the waterfront, watching the boats go by. Abhay was glad that she had finally decided to speak to him about whatever was bothering her. The mysterious WhatsApp messages had become a constant, unsettling hum beneath the surface of her days, a disquiet that had burrowed deep. Ever her anchor in the swirling currents of life, Abhay sat across from her, his gaze steady and reassuring. His caring nature had always been a balm to her soul, and now, more than ever, she needed his calm counsel.

A knot of confusion and a prickle of fear had taken root within her, a new and unwelcome sensation. Dipika. The name echoed in the silent spaces between Anjali's thoughts. Their shared history was a tangled web of whispered confidences and carefully constructed facades. Anjali had always been a loyal friend, a shield against the harsh realities Dipika seemed to attract. She had smoothed over the inconsistencies, defended the questionable choices, all the things one does for a friend.

But Dipika… Dipika was different. There was a fragility beneath the bravado, a desperate yearning for acceptance that manifested as a relentless performance of happiness and success in this glittering city. Anjali knew the truth: the quiet desperation of Dipika's isolated existence and the stark absence of a supportive family. She had witnessed the cracks in Dipika's carefully constructed world firsthand.

As the words tumbled out, a torrent of anxieties and veiled allusions, Anjali felt a sliver of the oppressive weight lift from her chest. Abhay listened intently, his brow furrowed in concern. "Someone close to you, Anjali," he murmured, his voice thoughtful. "It has to be someone in your immediate circle. Who else would know how to get under your skin like this?" Yet, as he looked into her eyes, he saw not just confusion, but a profound, visceral fear, a terror that hinted at secrets far darker than he could imagine.

"I did it for her, Abhay," she whispered, the words catching in her throat, the last of the amber liquid disappearing from her glass. He had noticed her increasing reliance on the numbing embrace of alcohol, a worrying trend that may have begun after Dipika's death. He loved Anjali deeply and cherished her strength and independence, but he had never glimpsed this shadowed corner of her life. He knew better than to push, to pry. Suffocation was the quickest way to lose Anjali. He would offer support, a safe harbour, without demanding entry into her private storm.

He reached across the small table, his hand covering hers. "This has to stop, babe." His voice was gentle but firm. "Are you absolutely sure you don't want to speak to Detective Razi Shufa? You told me he was helpful with the investigation after... after Dipika."

Anjali recoiled as if stung. "No! Absolutely not!" Her vehemence startled him. A cold dread began to seep into Abhay's heart. Her reaction's intensity and the raw panic in her eyes spoke volumes. How well did he truly know the woman whose hand he held, the woman he envisioned sharing his life with? The secrets Anjali harboured felt like a vast, uncharted territory, and suddenly, Abhay felt adrift, a stranger in the landscape of her inner world

She ignored his suggestion and instead recounted the details of the WhatsApp messages and then hesitantly shared Adil's bewildering words. "He said… he saw Dipika, Abhay. He said, 'She's back.' It was so real, so filled with fear. I mean …how could he have seen her?"

Abhay listened patiently, his brow furrowed with concern. "Anjali, are you sure he was lucid? He's been through so much. It could have been a hallucination, a side effect of the stroke or the medication."

"I don't know," Anjali admitted, her voice laced with uncertainty. "That's what's scaring me. First the message, and now this. It feels… connected."

Driven by a desperate need for answers, Anjali had even called Dipika's mother in Delhi. But Mansi aunty's response had been strangely detached. "Oh, hello beta. How are you all? Hope things are alright in Dubai. I'm just off to my bridge group, so I can't talk for long." Her breezy dismissal had left Anjali feeling even more anxious. How could she burden Dipika's grieving mother with such bizarre and unbelievable news – a cryptic message and Adil having a neurosurgery-induced hallucination about the sudden reappearance of her deceased daughter? It felt cruel and absurd.

"Someone knew how close I was to Dipika and only sent me that message, Abhay," Anjali said, her voice barely above a whisper. "And now Adil… it's like someone is playing a very twisted game."

Abhay reached for her hand, his touch firm and reassuring. "Relax, Anjali. It's probably just some sick individual trying to get a rise out of you, knowing your connection to what happened to Dipika. Adil is recovering from a severe head injury; his mind might be playing tricks on him. Don't let this consume you."

His calm logic offered a temporary reprieve and Anjali clung to his reassurances, trying to convince herself that it was all just a cruel coincidence, a figment of a disturbed mind or a malicious prank.

Returning to her apartment later that evening, a sliver of the anxiety had receded, replaced by a fragile sense of calm. But as she reached her door, her heart lurched. A folded piece of paper had been slipped underneath. Her fingers trembled as she picked it up and unfolded it. The message scrawled in harsh, uneven letters sent a fresh wave of icy dread through her veins:

"Bitch. return my money."

Chapter 21

Rupali and Rohit were buzzing with anticipation as they planned their upcoming trip to London, which promised to be a much-needed breath of fresh air. The relentless pace of Dubai life, coupled with the subtle but persistent anxieties of the past few months, had made the prospect of a getaway incredibly appealing.

However, beneath Rupali's excitement lay a layer of concern. Anjali had been acting withdrawn and unlike herself lately. A niggling feeling told Rupali that something was amiss, and she couldn't shake off the worry that Anjali was on the verge of a breakdown herself. "Maybe a change of scenery will do her good," Rupali mused, deciding to reach out. "Anjali, darling, Rohit and I are heading to London soon. Why don't you come shopping with me before we go? I need to pick up some things, and it would be lovely to have your company."

Part of Rupali's shopping agenda was dedicated to finding the perfect gifts for Karan's family. Anisha had painted a vivid picture of the Rawals – true aristocrats with impeccable taste and a long-standing lineage. Reva Rawal, Karan's mother, was apparently a significant figure in the UK's philanthropic circles, sitting on the boards of several prominent charities. Dr. Rishabh Rawal, Karan's father, was described as a leading ophthalmologist. Rupali wanted to ensure her gifts reflected her respect and admiration for them, hoping to make a good impression.

Meanwhile, Rohit was practically bursting with excitement. Anisha, it appeared, had truly found an exceptional partner in Karan. The stories she shared painted a picture of a sophisticated and influential family, a far cry from some of the more… colourful characters Rohit had to navigate in his business dealings.

Speaking of which, a knot of unease tightened in Rohit's stomach as he thought of Manish. His business partner had recently started exhibiting a disturbing level of curiosity regarding Raagastar's accounts. Replacing their long-standing, trusted accountant with someone from his father-in-law Kamal Gupta's company felt like a deliberate and unwelcome intrusion. Rohit found himself increasingly on edge.

The entertainment industry in the GCC was a complex web, and Rohit had learned early on that maintaining smooth operations required a delicate dance. Ensuring that international artists could perform without a hitch often involved navigating murky waters. Huge sums were at stake, and keeping everyone "happy" – from legitimate stakeholders to those operating in the shadows – was simply the cost of doing business. Deals with the underworld and discreet payments to various middlemen to secure coveted album rights were all part of the game that had propelled Raagastar to its current success.

But Manish's sudden demand for transparency, for a clear and open look at their books, was a dangerous proposition. It threatened to expose the very mechanisms that had fuelled their growth, the very secrets Rohit was most determined to keep hidden. The trip to London couldn't come soon enough for Rohit; a temporary escape from the mounting pressure and the unsettling scrutiny of his business. He hoped the change of scenery would offer some respite from the heat and allow him to strategise his next move.

Anjali and Rupali, meanwhile, were in their element, navigating the gleaming corridors of Dubai's most luxurious malls with infectious energy. The upcoming engagement of Anisha had unleashed their inner shopping divas, and they were on a mission to find the perfect gifts for both the bride-to-be and her in-laws, the Rawals. Their tastes were impeccable, a trait Anjali shared with Rupali, and their choices reflected it.

The boutiques in Bur Dubai yielded shimmering silks and exquisitely hand-embellished chiffon sarees, each a testament to intricate karigari work. Next, they ventured into high-end fashion havens, emerging with shopping bags filled with buttery soft cashmere stoles in a rainbow of hues, a pair of iconic Manolo Blahnik heels, and elegant pieces from Gucci and Dior. The sheer volume of their acquisitions grew to such an extent that Rupali, laughing, had to enlist the help of the mall concierge to have them all sent home. It was simply too much to be carrying it all home themselves.

Finally, amidst the delightful chaos, the girls paused for a much-needed coffee break. It was then that the festive atmosphere around Anjali seemed to dissipate. She turned to Rupali, her brow furrowed with worry. "I need to talk to you about the second message," she began, her voice lower than usual, recounting Adil's unsettling words. "It could be just a horrible prank, but why would a sick man invent such a story about someone he hasn't even spoken to in a year?"

A shadow crossed Anjali's face. "We've all moved on, Rupali. We don't want to be haunted by the past. And now, out of nowhere, this new drama is unfolding."

Rupali, ever the pragmatist, suggested, "Why don't you call Detective Razi Shufa?"

Anjali recoiled slightly. "Oh, I don't know. He'll ask a million questions, and honestly, I just don't have the time to deal with a whole new investigation right now."

Rupali was surprised. Anjali, usually so composed and in control, looked flustered and visibly angry. "Well," Rupali smiled, attempting to lighten the mood, "it seems like you might not have a choice but to deal with it when I get back from London. I have a wedding to plan, after all and I definitely need your help!"

"Of course, my darling…what could give me more pleasure?" laughed Anjali.

With a practised ease, she deftly changed the subject, her cheerful demeanour returning as if a switch had been flipped. What Rupali didn't know, Anjali reasoned, wouldn't hurt her. However, the weight of the unsettling message remained a hidden burden beneath the surface of the joyful shopping spree.

Chapter 22

Hand in hand, Karan Rawal and Anisha Jahangir stood at Heathrow's arrivals gate, a strikingly handsome couple radiating an easy charm. The young couple had arrived from New York the day before, in time to meet Anisha's parents when they arrived in London. They were undeniably well-matched, a picture of youthful success and quiet anticipation. Anisha, usually so self-assured, harboured a secret hope that her parents, Rupali and Rohit, would not only like Karan but also his family, the established Rawals of London. Having rarely denied their "princess" anything in her life, Anisha clung to the belief that this time would be no different.

Seven years had passed since Anisha left Dubai for university, forging an independent path that led her to a coveted position at a leading investment bank in New York. She had strived to make her parents proud, excelling academically and professionally. Now, her heart was set on marrying Karan. However, the few brief exchanges she'd had with Karan's parents had been formal, leaving a knot of worry in her stomach. How would these two families truly connect, one rooted in Dubai's self-made success and the other in London's generational wealth?

Karan, though part of the established Rawal lineage, was refreshingly down to earth and appeared to love Anisha genuinely. Their life together in New York was a testament to their shared ambition and willingness to build their future. Yet, the impending meeting in London felt significant, a bridge to be crossed. Despite her mother's warm congratulations over the phone, a persistent anxiety lingered in Anisha's mind. The harmony between the Jahangirs and the Rawals felt crucial, the very foundation upon which Anisha and Karan's future happiness would be built.

The sleek Emirates A380 touched down smoothly at Heathrow, its gentle rumble a familiar comfort to Rupali and Rohit as they disembarked and made their way through the bustling terminal. Excitement washed over them. It had been too long since they'd last seen Anisha.

Rounding the corner past customs, their eyes scanned the waiting crowd. And then they saw her – Anisha! Her radiant smile shone even brighter than they remembered, and beside her stood a handsome young man with a warm, welcoming gaze.

"Mom! Dad!" Anisha's voice was filled with joy as she rushed forward, enveloping them in tight hugs, first her mother, then her father.

"Anisha, my darling!" Rupali squeezed her daughter, tears welling up in her eyes. Rohit clapped Anisha on the back, a broad grin on his face.

"And this must be Karan," Rohit said, extending his hand towards the young man, standing somewhat hesitantly beside his daughter.

"Namaste, Uncle, Aunty," Karan replied, his handshake firm and friendly. "It's lovely to meet you both."

After warm introductions and excited chatter, Karan efficiently took charge of their luggage. "Right then," he announced, leading them towards the exit, "let's get you both settled in. We have a car waiting."

A sleek, chauffeur-driven car was indeed waiting just outside. Anisha and Karan settled into the back with Rupali and Rohit, the comfortable leather seats a welcome respite after their long flight. As they navigated the London streets, Anisha pointed out famous landmarks flashing by – a glimpse of the London Eye, the Houses of Parliament in the distance.

Although Rohit & Rupali had travelled to the UK several times, this trip was memorable and they were enjoying the experience of the kids leading the way for a change.

Soon, the car pulled up to a grand building, its elegant facade exuding an air of timeless luxury. The doorman, impeccably dressed, opened their door with a polite bow.

"Welcome to The Ritz Carlton, London," Anisha announced with a proud smile.

Rupali and Rohit exchanged impressed glances. With its opulent entrance and hushed elegance, the iconic hotel was even more magnificent in person.

"Oh, Anisha, this is… incredible!" Rupali exclaimed, taking in the grandeur of the lobby.

"I know you've been to London before, mummy, but we wanted this experience to be special," Anisha said, linking her arm with her mother's. Karan smiled warmly at Rohit as they followed the bellboy towards the check-in desk, ready to begin their London adventure in style.

Later that evening, Rupali and Rohit were abuzz with a nervous energy as they waited for the kids to pick them up. This evening was crucial. Meeting Karan's parents, Reva and Dr. Rishabh Rawal, felt like a significant milestone, a gateway into a world Rohit had only glimpsed from afar. The fact that Anisha's boyfriend hailed from such an esteemed lineage was not lost on him. He was genuinely impressed by all that he had read about Dr. Rawal, a leading ophthalmologist in the UK.

It was a stark contrast to his simmering disdain for Manish and his father-in-law, Kamal Gupta. The scrutiny of Raagastar's business operations was a constant worry for Rohit. He desperately needed a distraction, a grand spectacle to divert Manish Gupta's prying eyes. A lavish Desi wedding, the kind that would set tongues wagging across Dubai and London's elite circles, seemed like the perfect smokescreen. Rohit, a self-made man who had navigated the treacherous waters of Dubai's business world through sheer grit and calculated risks, was amazed at how naive Manish was. How did he imagine their company had snagged some of the biggest contracts with some of the most iconic artistes of their time?

Manish's greatest accomplishment was getting married to Naina Gupta. He was clearly clinging onto his father-in-law's wealth and influence, a stark contrast to Rohit's own hard-earned achievements.

As 7 pm approached, a palpable tension hung in the air of their luxurious hotel suite. When Rupali emerged from the bedroom, Rohit couldn't help but gasp. She looked breathtaking in a pale green evening gown, delicate seed pearls shimmering like captured moonlight against the flowing fabric. She resembled an ethereal mermaid, her grace and poise radiating effortlessly. Rohit, sharp in his impeccably tailored suit, felt a surge of pride. Together, they were a formidable pair, ready to make a lasting impression.

Anisha and Karan arrived promptly, their easygoing demeanour a slight contrast to the nervous anticipation swirling within Rupali and Rohit. "Just be yourself ma", she had said to Rupali over the phone earlier. "They're going to love you". Now, Rupali, for some reason, felt increasingly nervous. Rohit had the expression he usually wore when he was eager to impress a business prospect. "Would everything be reduced to a contract for this man?", she wondered sadly. Even the wedding of their only daughter! The drive to the Rawal mansion was filled with polite conversation, but beneath the surface, Rohit was mentally preparing himself for this important meeting. They had to impress the Rawal family.

Driving up to the Rawal residence was an experience in itself. The sheer scale of the property, the manicured gardens stretching into the twilight, spoke volumes of a wealth that dwarfed even their own considerable success. Yet, as they were ushered inside, Rohit was struck by the understated elegance of the interiors. There was no ostentatious display, just a quiet, assured sense of luxury. They were seated on an expensive-looking Cream and ebony sofa set that appeared to blend classic comfort with timeless sophistication and style. Rupali was awestruck by the Persian carpet in the centre of the room, which looked like the famed Clark Sickle-Leaf, a 17th-century antique Persian rug that had sold at a Sotheby's auction for 33 million US Dollars.

The rest of the room though held ebony book cases and grim looking wrought iron chairs. Even though it was an unusually warm summer's day, Rupali felt a chill creeping up her spine. It was all quite unfamiliar and overwhelming.

"Hello, hello Mr & Mrs Jahangir and welcome to London."

Reva Rawal greeted them with a polite but undeniably formal air. Her hairstyle, a severe, tight bun, accentuated the sparseness of her hair, drawing attention to her sharp, almost bony features and thin lips. Her attire was stark and austere, devoid of any embellishment. While she was outwardly hospitable, offering them cocktails and polite conversation, a distinct coldness emanated from her, a subtle distance that Rohit couldn't quite decipher.

Rupali, ever the gracious hostess even when not in her own home, presented Reva with the carefully chosen designer gifts she had brought from Dubai. Reva however accepted them with a curt nod, her eyes barely flicking over the luxurious packaging before placing them on a nearby table for one of the omnipresent help to discreetly take inside. Her lack of enthusiasm was palpable, a clear indication that material possessions held little sway over her.

Rohit observed everything intently, his mind racing. The Rawals were undoubtedly in a different league, their wealth seemingly ingrained, a part of their very being rather than something recently acquired. He knew this meeting was more than just a polite introduction; it was a silent assessment, a glimpse into the world his daughter would now be a part of. He was determined to navigate this social terrain with grace and ensure that Anisha's happiness was secured, even if it meant stepping outside his own comfort zone. The wedding, he knew, had to be perfect, a dazzling spectacle that would not only distract his business rivals but also earn him the respect of this formidable family.

The conversation took an unexpected turn when Reva, with a serene smile that still didn't quite thaw her sharp features, mentioned her involvement with the Art of Living. "It has brought such peace and clarity to my life," she stated, her tone almost a pronouncement. "And I encourage both Karan and Anisha to participate in the breathwork and daily yoga practices."

Rohit and Rupali exchanged surprised glances. This spiritual inclination was certainly not something they had anticipated from the seemingly aloof Mrs. Rawal.

Dr. Rishabh Rawal, a jolly, hearty man with a booming laugh that seemed to fill the room, chuckled. "Yes, I rescued this one just in time when she was quite breathless, you know!" he declared, winking broadly at Rupali. "Before she got completely lost in the… well, never mind." He chuckled again, leaving his statement hanging in the air as his wife stared into space a million miles away.

Several times throughout the evening, Rishabh made similar cryptic allusions about "rescuing" Reva, each time accompanied by a knowing look or a smile in her direction. Rupali's curiosity was piqued. Rescued from what? She was tempted to ask, but the subtle warning glares from Rohit, who seemed intent on maintaining a smooth and agreeable facade, kept her questions firmly lodged in her throat. Clearly, the seemingly perfect Rawal family had their own undercurrents and unspoken stories.

Reva, regaining control of the conversation, turned to Anisha with a formal smile that, despite the words, lacked genuine warmth. "Anisha, we are delighted to welcome you into our family."

Anisha, who had been unusually quiet, simply offered a polite smile in return. Rupali couldn't help but notice her daughter's attire – a simple, raw cotton co-ord set in a muted beige. It was a far cry from the vibrant colours Anisha had always favoured. A pang of concern went through Rupali; was her vivacious daughter already trying to dim her own light to align with her prospective mother in law's austere sensibilities?

"Yes," Reva continued, her gaze sweeping over them all, "the daily breathwork and yoga have been wonderful for all of us. Such a grounding influence in this chaotic world. I hope both of you have been keeping up your daily yoga routine in New York ".

Karan and Anisha both murmured their polite agreement.

As they finally settled around the large, impeccably set dining table, Karan, perhaps sensing the slightly stilted atmosphere, broached the subject of engagement plans. "So, Mom, Dad, Rupali Aunty, Rohit Uncle, Anisha and I have been talking…"

Before he could elaborate, Reva interjected, her tone leaving little room for discussion. "Yes, the engagement. It should be a small, intimate gathering. Close friends, like family. No more than twenty-five, certainly. A nice sit down dinner, a subtle announcement. We are not ones for loud, garish celebrations, and I sincerely hope that is not what you two have in mind." Her gaze rested pointedly on Karan and Anisha, leaving the pair dumbstruck.

Karan's father, Dr. Rishabh Rawal nodded his head sagely in agreement with his wife.

Rupali was utterly taken aback. A guest list of twenty-five for an engagement? In their Dubai circles, even a casual get together often exceeded that number. She glanced at Rohit, expecting him to at least offer a counter-suggestion, but to her astonishment, he was nodding in complete agreement, his eyes fixed on Reva with an almost deferential expression. Rupali was speechless, a knot of unease tightening in her stomach. This was not the grand, joyous celebration she had envisioned for her daughter. It seemed the Rawals had a very clear vision for everything, and Rohit, for reasons she couldn't yet fathom, was wholeheartedly endorsing it.

Why hadn't Anisha mentioned that her mother in law to be was straight out of the Addams family, thought Rupali, silently observing her daughter from across the table. She fervently hoped that Anisha knew what she was getting into.

"Of course we cannot move ahead with any of the engagement or wedding plans until we have the approval of "Bhai", said Reva almost reverently, staring into the distance and addressing an invisible stranger.. "Of course baby …of course said Dr. Rishabh softly crooning to his wife. "*Bhai ke bina kuch nahin hoga.*"

As Rupali and Rohit looked on uncomfortably, Karan interjected and said, "That's mom's brother Nanam uncle who has a home in Hampstead when he's here in London. He would love to meet you."

Chapter 23

"Anjali, you won't believe the kind of people Anisha has gotten involved with," Rupali's voice crackled over the phone line, a mixture of disbelief and frustration evident in her tone. "These Rawals… they are just so… so… weird!"

Anjali listened patiently as Rupali recounted the details of the dinner at the Rawal mansion, her voice rising in exasperation as she described Reva's austere demeanour, Rishabh's cryptic pronouncements, and the bizarre emphasis on breathwork and yoga.

"And Rohit! It's maddening, Anjali! He's just nodding along to everything they say, letting them completely take the lead. You'd think he was trying to win some kind of approval contest. And poor Anisha… she's like a little mouse, too scared to utter a single protest. Gone is my independent, opinionated daughter!" Rupali lamented.

Anjali sighed softly. "Go with the flow for now, sweetheart," she advised gently. "Perhaps once the London engagement is done, the Rawals might be more amenable to a bigger celebration in Dubai. Let's not jump to conclusions just yet."

The conversation then shifted to happenings in Dubai, a familiar and comforting topic. Rupali was relieved to hear that Adil was recovering well, thanks in no small part to Pam's unwavering support. The news of Sakina's newfound kindness towards her husband after his illness brought a small smile to Rupali's face. Some good could come out of adversity, it seemed. Hopefully she would now get over her obsession with Rohit and concentrate on her own marriage!

Anjali remained conspicuously silent about the happenings in her own life, offering only vague assurances that she was "fine." Rupali sensed a reticence, a shadow in her friend's voice, but refrained from pressing for more details. She knew Anjali would share more when she was ready. Little did Rupali know that Anjali was battling a silent tormentor, someone who was deliberately preying on her grief over Dipika, causing sleepless nights and a gnawing anxiety. She decided to wait until Rupali returned from London to confide in her, not wanting to burden her friend with more worries when she already had Anisha's peculiar in-laws to contend with.

Anjali also told Rupali how sweet Naina had been lately, supporting her with everything that needed to be done for Sakina & Adil and generally being there for her as a good friend.

"You know, Anjali," Rupali said, a hint of surprise in her voice, "we were so wrong about Naina Gupta."

"Tell me about it!" Anjali chuckled. "She's been an absolute rock. So loyal and supportive."

Rupali was genuinely delighted. Naina had always projected an air of aloofness, a certain snootiness that had kept them at arm's length. To hear that she was showing such a different side was a pleasant surprise. "I'm so happy to hear that," Rupali said warmly. "It's good to know she has such a good heart." She had always thought Naina Gupta was terribly spoilt. It was certainly refreshing to see this side of her.

"We should all get together when you're back," Anjali suggested. "Let's meet Naina for tea at that new Tiffany Blue café in Emirates mall. It'll be just like old times – you, me, Sakina, and now Naina to complete our foursome."

Rupali's spirits lifted at the thought. A reunion with her closest friends, a return to the familiar comfort of Dubai, was exactly what she needed after this unsettling foray into the strange world of the Rawals. "That sounds perfect, Anjali. I'll let you know as soon as I'm back".

The next morning, Anisha came alone to pick her parents up and take them sightseeing. It was a welcome break from the strangely formal world of the Rawals.

Rohit seemed relieved as well. They had agreed that they would meet Karan's uncle in Hampstead that evening for tea. Anisha reassured them that it was merely a formality.

"Reva aunty has barely any contact with her brother ma. Rishabh uncle married her ages ago. Infact Karan says his only memories of his uncle are of him sending him toys and chocolates and several gifts over the years, wherever he was. Apparently he runs some global media business….anyway that's all I know.. I haven't met him either."

The drive to Nanam uncle's Hampstead residence was a study in contrasts. Rohit, practically vibrating with anticipation, peppered Rupali with cheerful conjectures about Reva's powerful brother. Rupali, however, was more attuned to the quiet tension emanating from Anisha in the back seat. Her daughter's unusually subdued demeanour made Rupali hesitate to probe. It was likely the prospect of meeting Karan's London family for the first time, a situation that could easily overwhelm a young girl.

As they pulled up at the sprawling Hampstead mansion, the sheer number of staff milling about the entrance struck them both. Dressed uniformly in black suits and dark glasses, they exuded an air of formidable efficiency. "Personal staff or bodyguards?" Rohit murmured, his initial ebullience slightly tempered by the imposing scene.

The Rawals arrived shortly after in their own silver Rolls Royce Phantom, their expressions unreadable. Inside, the palatial drawing room was opulent and yet strangely heavy with unspoken tension. Karan, attempting to lighten the atmosphere, offered a few strained jokes about London traffic, but his efforts fell flat against the palpable sense of foreboding.

Reva's voice, when she finally spoke, was thick with emotion. "Nanam is my everything. He's more than my brother, my parents to me. I would be nowhere without him." Dr. Rishabh offered a soft murmur of agreement, gently squeezing her hand. Rupali couldn't shake a disquieting feeling, a nagging thought about potential family eccentricities. Rohit, ever the diplomat, smiled kindly at Reva and then went on to respond to Karan's jokes with hearty laughter, projecting an image of easygoing friendliness.

A sudden flurry of movement near the entrance announced his arrival as "Nanam" entered the room, an imposing figure of a middle-aged man, large and overweight, draped in black and glittering with gold chains bearing talismans. His fingers were adorned with a large ruby and an equally impressive emerald ring. Flanked by the black-suited entourage, his voice raspy and hoarse boomed a greeting. "Reva, my sister, my little sparrow – come here, my *Jaan*. My darling little princess. How are you?"

Reva rushed into his expansive embrace, whimpering, "Nanam... Nanam... my *Bhai*." He settled heavily into a large armchair at the centre of the room, his gaze slowly sweeping across the room, taking in each of them. "Karan," he said, his voice surprisingly gentle as he gestured to Karan to come over to him and ruffled his hair, "I always knew you were a smart boy. And Anisha... God has blessed her infinitely, my child," he added, his eyes lingering on the bride to be.

The Jahangirs exchanged a hesitant glance, unsure of the appropriate form of address. Before they could utter a word,"Nanam" suddenly narrowed his eyes, fixing his gaze directly on Rohit. " I hear you're from Dubai. I have many friends there. Know the place very well.

Have we met before, Mr. Jahangir?" he asked, his voice now carrying a sharp edge. "My name is Nadim Sheikh!"

A jolt of recognition, sharp and terrifying, shot through Rohit. Of course that's who he was.. Nadim Sheikh! The name echoed in the corridors of the music underworld, a realm where he wielded immense power, his influence stretching across global artists. No major show in the Middle East could proceed without his tacit approval, his pockets lined with payoffs. Rohit's Dubai contacts, the middlemen he'd dealt with for years, were Sheikh's men. But to stand face-to-face with the man himself, to feel the weight of his presence, was a chilling revelation.

As Anisha, following Karan's earlier instruction, rose respectfully to touch Nanam *mamu*'s feet, Rohit felt a wave of dismay. Nadim Sheikh was not just an influential figure; he was a Don. Any alliance with this family would undoubtedly come at a steep price.

"It's a pleasure, Mr. Sheikh," Rohit managed to stammer out, his jovial facade crumbling. "Actually, I do *not* believe we have ever met."

Chapter 24

The usually talkative Rohit was a study in silence on their return journey. Rupali, attributing his unusual quietude to the undeniably peculiar situation related to Karan's family, gently squeezed his hand. "Everything will be fine, Rohit," she offered, her voice soft with reassurance.

But Rohit was far away, lost in the echoing chambers of his past. The prospect of forging an alliance with Nadim Sheikh, a union cemented by his daughter's marriage into the Rawal family, felt like a public endorsement of criminality. The implications for Raagastar were terrifying. What would Manish Gupta, Kamal Gupta, and the other shareholders say if they ever discovered the true price of those lucrative music contracts, the exclusive rights to the biggest artists? He had foolishly believed it was the only way to claw his way out of past financial woes, a desperate gamble that had now sprung a monstrous trap.

Refusing this alliance, however, was equally unthinkable. He had seen the genuine affection in Anisha's eyes for Karan; to deny her happiness would be to alienate her forever. And the truth, the ugly, compromising truth, was a secret he couldn't afford to share with his family, under any circumstances. A heavy cloak of deception weighed him down. He had worked relentlessly for his success, and now it teetered precariously on the brink of ruin.

He glanced at Rupali, elegant and composed beside him, and then at Anisha, his beautiful, accomplished daughter sitting quietly in the back seat. How would his past actions taint their future?

Having agreed to stay in touch with Karan's parents and tentatively plan an engagement in the autumn in London, followed by a December wedding in Dubai, the Jahangirs were finally en route to the airport, their flight back to Dubai looming. Rohit's mind raced, a frantic whirlwind of damage control. Perhaps Reva Rawal's seemingly austere nature and her expressed wish for a low-key wedding could be a blessing in disguise, a way to minimise the inevitable scandal within their social circles. He would have to carefully persuade Rupali of the same. Once the children were married, perhaps Nadim Sheikh could be... managed, kept at a distance, his influence diluted by the vast expanse of the ocean separating them between the UK and the US. The thought offered a sliver of fragile hope in the suffocating darkness of his predicament.

Chapter 25

The flight back to Dubai had been a blur, a metal tube hurtling through the sky while Rohit's mind remained trapped in the opulent, yet chilling, drawing room of Nadim Sheikh's London residence. The casual mention of "Nanam" by Mrs. Rawal, the easy familiarity in Reva's voice – it all replayed in his head with the sickening clarity of a nightmare. The odds, the sheer improbability of their paths colliding in such a personal and consequential way, felt like a cruel twist of fate. Nadim Sheikh. A phantom in the music industry, a name whispered with a mixture of fear and grudging respect. His empire, built on foundations shrouded in secrecy, stretched across continents, his influence undeniable, his methods…unspoken. Rohit had always maintained a careful distance, doing his business with representatives, but never direct engagement with the man himself. Now, the man would be family. It was a thought that filled him with dread.

The cheerful lilt in Anisha's voice during their video call from New York was in sharp contrast to the turmoil churning within him. "Dad, you liked them, right? Karan's parents were kind of sweet no?!" Her eagerness for his approval, for the reassurance that everything was falling into place, twisted the knife deeper. He had forced a smile, a hearty "Of course, beta, they were lovely," while the memory of the strained silence that had descended after their visit to "Nanam's" house hung heavy in the air. Anisha, perceptive as she was, had noticed. He could see the fleeting question in her eyes before her parents had left the UK.

Losing Anisha was an unbearable thought. She was the axis around which his and Rupali's world revolved, their only child, cherished beyond measure. Yet, the joy of her impending marriage was now poisoned by the dread of what lay ahead. How could he reconcile his daughter's future with the looming shadow of Karan's uncle's reputation? What would his friends, his business associates, his entire social circle say when the truth inevitably surfaced? The whispers, the knowing glances, the unspoken judgements – he could already feel them like icy tendrils wrapping around him.

A cold sweat broke out on his forehead as the most terrifying thought took root: would they believe he had orchestrated this? Had he, knowingly or unknowingly, walked his precious daughter into the heart of a dangerous web? The very notion was abhorrent, yet the circumstances were damning.

The weight of his professional life added to the crushing pressure. Manish Gupta's increasing scrutiny of Raagastar's finances felt less like routine diligence and more like a predator circling its prey. How long before questions were raised, uncomfortable connections were made, and his position as CEO became untenable? Would this scandal be the catalyst that finally brought his carefully constructed career crashing down?

Arriving back at their home in Dubai, Rohit refused any food and quickly retreated to his study claiming he had work to finish. His expression had been terse ever since they left London and Rupali knew better than to probe. Best to leave him alone, she thought. She was exhausted herself and couldn't wait to take a shower and have a quick sandwich before she retreated to their bedroom done up in soothing sage green furnishings. Her migraine was killing her, and was worsened by the jetlag, she just had to take a nap.

Rohit stared out of the window of his study, the familiar Dubai skyline offering no comfort. He was caught in an impossible bind, a suffocating dilemma where his past dealings threatened his present happiness and his future security. For the first time in his life, the path ahead was shrouded in a terrifying uncertainty. The man who had always prided himself on his strategic thinking, his ability to navigate complex situations, was now adrift, lost in a sea of his own making, desperately searching for a lifeline that seemed increasingly out of reach.

Barely a few kilometres away from Rohit, sitting in her office Anjali Sen was facing a dilemma of her own. The messages from "Dipika" would not allow her to rest in peace. She constantly wondered whether Sakina and Rupali were lying to her. If the person sending these messages out, referring to the money, was truly an impostor, they would have sent the messages out to all of Dipika's friends, hoping that some secrets would come tumbling out regarding her finances. However, both Sakina and Rupali had denied ever receiving any such messages, and Anjali was inclined to believe them. This could only mean one thing – that the secrets that Dipika had shared with her and her alone were now somehow known to another person. It was as if it were yesterday, the way Dipika's soulful brown eyes had pleaded with Anjali, a silent, desperate entreaty for understanding. *Anju di... you have to help me. I have no one else I can trust.* The quiet ominousness of her voice still echoed in Anjali's mind.

Dippy, her Dippy, the darling so often misjudged by their circle of friends.

The label of 'drifter' had clung to Dipika, unkindly bestowed upon her by those who saw only the surface. The lack of a visible career, a romantic partner, or defined passions painted a picture of aimlessness in their eyes. Her often-dank hair and generally unkempt appearance only solidified their shallow judgments. But Anjali knew better. She had been the confidante, the keeper of Dipika's secrets, the one person Dippy consistently turned to.

Now, in the stark light of Dipika's unexplained death, a chilling realisation washed over Anjali. Despite their long history, how little she truly knew about the intricate tapestry of Dipika's life. Her passing had ripped open a Pandora's box, unleashing a diabolical plot that had not only claimed Dipika but had also fractured the very foundations of their friendships. Even with the detailed investigation that followed, a crucial piece of the puzzle remained elusive, a secret Dipika had carried with her to the grave.

Anjali's thoughts drifted back to those final weeks, the palpable unease radiating from Dipika." *Mama always wanted me to come back to Delhi and live with her. To leave Dubai forever. But I absolutely don't want to do that.*" The words, laced with a raw anguish, resonated in Anjali's memory. *Delhi brings back the most painful memories of my childhood... of losing Dad... of losing...* Dipika's voice had choked, the unspoken grief a heavy weight in the air. Anjali had instinctively pulled her close, offering silent comfort.

Mansi aunty. Dipika's elderly mother in Delhi. That was her biggest worry, Dipika had confided. "*Mummy has only her trusted servants with her right now.*" The image

Dipika painted was of a woman fading, a stark contrast to the vibrant socialite Anjali remembered. *She's always been so completely independent, so full of life. Between dressing up for her bridge matches at the club and parties at the Delhi Gymkhana club, she barely had any time for Dad when he was alive, nor for me.* Anjali could almost see Mansi aunty in her mind's eye, a vision of elegance in flowing chiffon sarees of every imaginable hue, a string of pearls gracing her neck, her sparkling presence effortlessly drawing people to her.

Ageing has not been kind to her, Dipika had said, her voice tinged with sadness. *She is now a frail and very diminished version of herself. She cannot remember the simplest things – who lent her a book the previous week, the simplest recipes she's made at least a million times.* The details Dipika had shared painted a heartbreaking picture. *Our cousin Rommy wrote to me last week to say that mummy had forgotten how to grate cheese for a sandwich. She stared blankly at the grater, asking Rommy again and again what his favourite food was. Rommy described the situation as being really sad and helpless. No one could believe they were seeing Mansi aunty like this."*

The weight of Dipika's anxieties, the unspoken fears that had clouded her final days, pressed down on Anjali, as vivid and real as if it were yesterday. The desperate look in those soulful brown eyes, the quiet plea for help from an only child who was watching her parent sink into the depths of dementia – these were the fragments that haunted her, the echoes of a friendship tragically cut short, leaving behind a chasm of unanswered questions and a heart heavy with what might have been.

Suddenly, Detective Inspector Razi Shufa's face materialised in Anjali's mind—the genial, humorous police detective who had unravelled the enigma of Dipika's tragic end.

"Oh what a tangled web we weave, when first we practise to deceive," his voice echoed, quoting Walter Scott. A shiver ran down Anjali's spine. Why was she recalling that particular line so vividly? Was it meant for her? The thought troubled her, her lips tightening into a terse line as she abruptly shut down her laptop.

Chapter 26

Back in the familiar bustle of Dubai, Rupali immersed herself in domesticity, a welcome distraction from the unsettling London trip. Helping Sakina organise a girls' afternoon tea with Anjali, Naina, and herself offered a comforting return to routine. Adil's improving health was a shared relief, and the tea promised a much-needed respite from the recent drama.

Pamela, Adil's striking cousin, continued to be an invaluable support, but Sakina remained strangely resistant to Rupali's suggestion of including her in their tea gathering. "What can I say," Sakina explained quietly to Rupali, a hint of weariness in her voice. "Pam is just... too perfect at everything. It gets exhausting after a while. Makes me feel utterly useless. Adil won't even decide what to have for breakfast without her input."

What Sakina kept hidden from Rupali was the resurgence of a far more sinister problem than "Perfect Pam." Ali Rez, Adil's ex-boss, was relentlessly pursuing their affair, his advances only temporarily halted by Adil's accident and hospitalisation. Now, with Adil on the mend, Sakina found herself constantly fabricating excuses for the unwelcome gifts that materialised at their apartment – Wimbledon tickets arriving unsolicited, late-night calls from London when Ali assumed her husband was asleep. His besotted behaviour was almost comical, if it weren't so deeply disturbing. Did he truly believe Adil was oblivious?

It pained Sakina to observe her husband's vacant gaze, his expressions often unreadable. Was it merely the lingering effects of his memory loss, or had he truly ceased to care? The ambiguity was a constant torment.

"You've got to stop this," Sakina hissed furiously into her phone during one of Ali's unwelcome calls. "It's making me feel like an escort... not your potential life partner, Ali! Give me some time to figure my circumstances out."

"And when is that likely to be?" he retorted, his voice laced with an ominous undertone. He was unaccustomed to being rebuffed by a woman, but Sakina... Sakina was no ordinary woman. She was a goddess in his eyes, breathtakingly beautiful and deserving of worship. In bed, she was a whirlwind of sensuality and passion, making him feel a youthful vitality he hadn't experienced in years. He had memorised every inch of her – the golden hue of her skin, the endless expanse of her tanned legs, the delicate beauty spot on the nape of her neck, the butterfly tattoo just above her breast. Sakina Nawaz would be his wife; he desired no other and would stop at nothing to make it happen. She now held a strange and potent control over him, transforming him into a man he barely recognised.

Sakina felt the undeniable weight of her influence. The seductress within her had not lost its power. "Be patient, my darling," she purred into the phone, her voice a silken web. "I've got it all figured out. Just give me some time. I will be yours and yours alone."

Sakina was no fool. She had learned the art of manipulation out of necessity long ago. Giving in to Ali's lecherous advances in London had felt like her only option when they were trapped and vulnerable. But this was

Dubai, her city, her home for over two decades. He was the outsider here, not her. She knew precisely the words and actions required to control the repulsive fool. Who did he think he was, treating her like some cheap conquest? Very soon, he would understand exactly why Sakina Nawaz was considered extraordinary, why she was whispered about in social circles as "the diva." They had weathered a storm since their return, but she would ensure she regained control. Their very survival depended on it.

The decision was unanimous: afternoon tea with the girls was planned at Tiffany Blue, a brilliant tea-house addition to the iconic store nestled within the sprawling grandeur of the Dubai mall. As always, Rupali's organisational touch transformed the simple plan into an exquisite affair. The environs were a perfect robin-egg blue, a calming and sophisticated backdrop to the gleaming silver cutlery and delicate fine china tea service. A subtle fragrance of roses hung in the air, a gentle complement to the delicate tea sandwiches and miniature pastries arranged on tiered stands.

As Rupali savoured a sip of her perfectly brewed Earl Grey, a sense of tranquillity washed over her. Afternoon tea was, for the discerning residents of Dubai, a cherished ritual – an opportunity to observe the world go by and engage in leisurely conversation over delectable treats. It was a far cry from the hurried caffeine fix at the ubiquitous Baristas and an appointment to be savoured. Dubai, indeed, boasted a collection of tea houses and cafes that were as aesthetically pleasing as they were indulgent, each one a potential Instagram favourite in these days of

#Like Share Repeat!

"Gosh, it's been ages since we did this," Rupali said, her smile encompassing the ladies gathered around her. In the days when Dipika was alive and their other dear friend Monika was still in Dubai, this had been their cherished routine – a luxurious spa treatment followed by an elegant afternoon tea. It had felt heavenly, a simple contentment with life's finer pleasures. Rupali, Sakina, Anjali, Dipika, and Monika – the "fabulous five," as they affectionately called themselves. Friendships forged over two decades in the city they all loved. They had shared their deepest secrets, offering unwavering support to one another... or so they had believed, until Dipika's tragic and suspicious death had shattered their idyllic world, a victim of cruel treachery.

Looking at Sakina, Anjali, and Naina now, a strange wave of déjà vu washed over Rupali, quickly followed by a quiet reassurance. However unconventional their current reality might appear to outsiders, they were moving forward, at their own pace. She felt a particular gratitude for Naina Gupta's presence. Dressed in a chic white linen dress, the unmistakable scent of Elie Saab clinging to her, Naina was proving to be a genuine pleasure to know. Her long, heartfelt conversations with Anjali had fostered a deep understanding and respect for all the women, even the often-guarded Sakina. They were not just survivors; these were women who had learned to stand tall, for themselves and for each other. How she wished their paths had crossed sooner.

Looking across at Rupali, Naina offered a gentle smile, consciously pushing aside thoughts of Rupali's debonair and flamboyant husband, Rohit Jahangir. These were women who truly deserved her friendship. Sakina had been profoundly grateful for Naina's unwavering support during Adil's illness, and Anjali was equally thankful for her presence in their lives. While none of the girls shared the same level of trust with Naina as they did with each other, they all recognised Naina's sincere efforts, and for now, that was enough.

Chapter 27

The afternoon unfolded beautifully, a tapestry woven with light-hearted banter and shared laughter. Rupali, fresh from the somewhat surreal experience of London society, regaled her friends with tales of the stiff formality of the Rawals and her constant feeling of being amidst a never-ending London fashion Week. Having heard about the seemingly austere Reva, Anjali quipped about needing to ensure her outfit for any future meeting would be crafted from hemp and adhere strictly to sustainable fashion principles, all in a bid to impress the formidable Mrs. Rawal. It was a curious truth, Anjali mused, that in the realm of the super-wealthy, less was often demonstrably more.

Beneath the surface of Anjali's cheerful demeanour, however, a gnawing anxiety persisted. The sleepless nights continued, punctuated by the unsettling ping of accusatory WhatsApp messages from the unknown intruder. The messages contained shocking details about all of them – their hidden pasts, secrets that seemingly only Dipika could have known. But Dipika was dead... or was she? The thought, unbidden and terrifying, flickered through Anjali's mind. She felt as if she were teetering on the edge of madness, desperately needing this torment to cease. But who could she trust enough to confide in?

She yearned for her friend…the Adil of the past, the man who had always been her anchor, her voice of reason, offering sound advice in every conceivable situation. She desperately wanted to discuss this disturbing situation with him, even more so than with her closest girlfriends. But the Adil she knew was gone, replaced by a polite stranger who offered only blank stares and stilted conversation, as if meeting her for the very first time. Sakina's strict instructions forbade her from causing him even the slightest stress, fearing a setback to his fragile health after his miraculous recovery from the head injury. She longed for a moment alone with him, away from Sakina's watchful eye and Pamela's ever-present scrutiny. What did Adil know? Had he been trying to communicate something to her in those frantic moments before he collapsed in Jumeirah?

Dipika had been a client of ABQ bank during her time in Dubai. Anjali clung to the hope that Adil, in his professional capacity, might possess some clue, some overlooked detail, that could shed light on who was behind these menacing threats. The repeated references to money were particularly troubling. Of course, the money had belonged to Dipika, and Dipika alone. But Dipika was gone.

A seed of suspicion, unwelcome and unsettling, began to sprout in Anjali's mind as she looked at her friends. Sultry Sakina, sophisticated Rupali, the seemingly pampered heiress Naina? Could it be that one of them knew more than they were letting on? The thought sent a shiver of unease down her spine, casting a shadow over the comforting warmth of their afternoon tea.

Oblivious to the dark currents swirling within Anjali's mind, the girls chattered animatedly about their delightful tea outing. Sakina, suddenly radiating a confidence and cheerfulness reminiscent of her pre-debacle "diva" persona, announced her intention to browse the Bloomingdale's sale in the mall. Aware of their friend's recent financial constraints, Rupali and Naina exchanged bemused glances, a silent acknowledgement of Sakina's seemingly newfound optimism. There was no denying Sakina's captivating allure – her vibrant reddish-brown hair, glowing complexion, and curvaceous yet slender figure were undeniably striking, especially accentuated by the carefully chosen peach linen dress that showcased her assets. In the wake of Adil's stroke, the awkwardness surrounding Sakina's ill-fated party had thankfully faded into unspoken history; her friends were determined to ensure her continued welcome within their Dubai circle.

As the girls made their way out of the café, their cheery exit was interrupted by a photographer who politely requested a few pictures for the Tiffany Blue café's ongoing social media campaign. Amused, Sakina instantly agreed, while Anjali made a hurried excuse about needing to return to work that afternoon. Rupali and Naina, sensing Anjali's discomfort followed suit also remembering pressing engagements elsewhere. Naina, in particular, bristled at the intrusion on their private outing. "So rude and inconsiderate," she murmured softly to Rupali as they said goodbyes hastily to Sakina. "I detest it when these fashion photographers accost you like that. Absolutely no privacy. I had half a mind to report that idiot to the mall security." Rupali, while finding the request harmless, had no intention of challenging Naina's strong opinion, acutely aware of Raagastar's reliance on her father's financial backing – a fact she couldn't afford to forget, even as their friendship deepened.

In stark contrast, Sakina was utterly delighted by the photographer's attention. The next hour or so was spent posing for his camera, his enthusiastic compliments about her natural talent and striking presence fuelling her burgeoning confidence. He told her that she was exactly the kind of glamorous, self-assured, and photogenic woman that brands were looking out for social media collaborations. He even offered to share her pictures with contacts at his agency, potentially connecting her with lucrative opportunities. Sakina was surprised by how easily she was able to follow his directions and how much genuine fun she was having. Why had she never considered modelling before? In this digital age, it seemed so simple to post a few captivating pictures with catchy captions on her own Instagram account. "You just need to be yourself – that's what people love the most," he advised. "Be brave, authentic, and fearless. I promise you, you'll be the rage before you know it."

Sakina was captivated. As she finally left the mall, a new and exciting possibility turned over and over in her mind – a potential career she had never even considered, suddenly presented to her with such encouraging ease.

Sakina's fingers danced across the cool glass of her phone, the soft glow illuminating the determined set of her jaw. Adil's gentle snores drifted from the bedside table, a comforting counterpoint to the burgeoning excitement thrumming within her. The photographer's words echoed in her mind: "Your earthy style…easy for people to connect with." And the photos! They were breathtaking, capturing a raw sensuality she hadn't fully recognised within herself before. They felt like the key to unlocking something new.

Hours melted away as Sakina navigated the labyrinth of Instagram. What had once been a casual space for sharing snippets of life with friends now felt like a vast, uncharted territory brimming with potential. She meticulously studied the profiles of established influencers, dissecting their captions, analysing their aesthetics, and trying to decipher the elusive algorithm that seemed to dictate their reach. She noted the artful composition of their photos, the engaging questions they posed, and the authentic way they seemed to connect with their followers.

A thrill coursed through her. This wasn't just about pretty pictures; it was about crafting a narrative, building a community. The thought of stepping out from behind the scenes, of finally having a platform to express herself and perhaps even earn a living, ignited a spark of fierce determination within her. She was tired of the quiet corners of life; it was time for her voice to be heard, her presence felt.

Sakina scrolled through her own modest Instagram feed, a collection of casual snapshots and fleeting moments. It was a blank canvas, waiting for her to paint her vision upon it. Tonight, the seeds of a new identity would be sown. She wouldn't just be another face in the digital crowd. She would be Sakina, and she would carve out a space that was uniquely hers, a space that resonated, captivated, and lingered in the minds of those who encountered it. This wasn't just a whim; it was a vow to herself. Her time to shine had arrived, and Sakina was more than ready to embrace it. She shared a picture of herself from the afternoon shoot, standing against the backdrop of the iconic Dubai fountains, her hair glistening in the afternoon sunshine, her smile as mesmeric as ever as she stared fearlessly into the camera, her eyes speaking volumes.

#Thisis me. #New beginnings

Chapter 28

Ali Rez's foot tapped a relentless rhythm against the polished floor of his hotel room. "Sakina, for heaven's sake! How much longer are you going to wait? Adil being unwell is becoming a convenient excuse. You need to tell him. Now." His voice, though hushed, carried a sharp edge of exasperation.

Sakina wrung her hands, her gaze fixed on a distant point and not the heavy set man in front of her. "Ali, you don't understand. He's truly not well. The doctor said any significant shock could..." Her voice trailed off, the unspoken words hanging heavy in the air. "I just need a little more time."

"Time for what, Sakina? For the distance between you and Adil to become an unbridgeable chasm?" Ali's tone softened slightly, but his impatience remained palpable. "Every day you delay is another day you're living a lie. And look at you! You're fading away in this house, watching his cousin take over your life."

Sakina flinched. He was right about that part at least.

The arrival of Pamela Chaudhry in their Dubai life felt less like a blessing and more like a swift, stylish takeover, leaving Sakina feeling increasingly like a shadow in her own home. Pam, Adil's vivacious and undeniably stunning cousin from New York, had descended like a perfectly tailored whirlwind, stepping in with an efficiency and confidence that Sakina couldn't help but find both helpful and deeply intimidating.

Pam's very presence seemed to radiate success. Her tales of private jet commutes across continents and high-stakes boardroom battles, splashed across news headlines, painted a stark contrast to Sakina's quieter life. The offer of a luxurious apartment in Dubai Hills, accepted with grateful relief by both Adil and Sakina, had been the first tangible sign of Pam's influence. "He's my brother," Pam had declared, tossing her glossy hair with an air of effortless generosity. "Obviously, I will help you guys. There's no two ways about that."

Yet, this generosity came with an unspoken assertion of control. Soon, two maids and a driver were bustling around their new home, their loyalties clearly lying with "Pamela madam." The medical arrangements for Adil's recovery, the 24-hour nurses, all meticulously orchestrated by Pam. Whenever Sakina attempted to assert herself, to offer her own care or opinion, Pam's gaze would sharpen with a subtle contempt. "We have no idea what caused Bhai to suddenly collapse like that, Sakina," she'd say, her tone laced with a thinly veiled accusation. "This time around, we need to be very careful and ensure he isn't upset by anything at all." Sakina had repeated several times that it was an accidental fall but Pam ignored that fact.

A gnawing suspicion began to take root in Sakina's mind – the feeling of being watched, of her privacy being invaded. She couldn't shake the unsettling feeling that Pam was tapping their phones. Adil, often lost in a haze of medication, remained oblivious. But Sakina had noticed the subtle shift in Pam's demeanour during their private conversations, a certain knowing glint in her eyes, a sharper edge to her voice.

The chilling thought slithered into her consciousness: had Pam listened to her conversations with Ali? Had her affair, a secret she desperately wanted to bury, somehow surfaced? And if so, how much had Pamela revealed to Adil? The idea of this seemingly ruthless woman, wielding such knowledge, sent a shiver of fear down Sakina's spine.

Despite the complexities of their relationship and the pain of her infidelity, Sakina had no intention of leaving Adil and certainly not for his ex-boss, Ali Rez. Alone, she believed, they could navigate their differences, rebuild their fractured trust. But fate, in the form of Pamela's unwavering presence and subtle manipulations, seemed determined to deny her that chance, casting a long, ominous shadow over her future

There was no doubt that Pam's efficient takeover of Adil's care had been swift and complete. There was barely anything left for Sakina to do. Pam managed his medication, his meals, even his conversations, leaving Sakina feeling like an unwelcome guest in her own home. And Adil... he was a shadow of his former self, lost in a world of his own thoughts, a constant furrow in his brow. The silence between them was thick with unspoken words, a testament to their growing estrangement.

Later that day, Sakina reached out to Anjali, hoping for some solace. "Anjali," she began, her voice heavy with worry, "Adil seems so lost, so deeply troubled. I try to talk to him, but he just stares blankly. And Pam... she's everywhere."

But Anjali's usual comforting tone was absent. " Don't be silly Sakina, Pam genuinely wants to help you guys.

After all she's family. Stop reading meaning into all these things. Thank God she's there and willing to help.

"Listen …" she said suddenly lowering her voice. "I... I have to tell you about something worrying me too." Her voice was tight with anxiety. "I'm still getting these strange messages. They won't stop. Whoever it is keeps mentioning Dipika... I mean who can be so vile. She is no more."

Sakina frowned. "Dipika? The messages haven't stopped yet? Have you said anything about this to Mansi aunty?"

No...of course not, said Anjali. She's too old and will be terribly upset.

"The worst part is that the messages are... they're accusatory," she whispered, trying hard to hide the tremor in her voice. "Saying I know more than I let on about what happened to her. Absolutely ridiculous. Who would do such a cruel thing?" A deep sigh escaped her lips. "It's just... who on earth could be so evil?"

Anjali finally told Sakina about the threats to pay back the money. This was not just a random person playing a stupid prank. This was someone who knew far more than they should about her and Dipika.

Sakina's own turmoil momentarily receded, replaced by a surge of concern for her friend. "Anjali, that's awful! Have you told anyone else?"

"Not yet," Anjali replied, her voice barely a whisper. "I don't know what to do."

Anjali Sen. The name itself conjured images of unwavering strength and quiet brilliance for her Dubai circle. She wasn't just a friend; she was the bedrock, the one they all leaned on. Her impeccable integrity was legendary, a guiding star in their lives. They watched with admiration as she carved her path, ultimately blossoming into the powerhouse editor of *Dubai Glam*, a testament to her sharp intellect and unwavering dedication.

Sakina, her brow furrowed with concern, knew Dipika held a unique place in Anjali's heart. Their bond ran deeper than the others, woven with shared secrets and unspoken understanding. If anyone had confided in Anjali about something so grave, so unsettling, it would have been Dipika.

Yet, the very notion of someone daring to accuse Anjali of financial impropriety, especially concerning their deceased friend, felt like a punch to the gut. It was utter madness, a vile accusation that Sakina instinctively knew to be false. Anjali? Siphoning money? From Dipika? It was an impossibility, a stain on Anjali's character that Sakina refused to believe.

After all Anjali was a successful professional in her own right. She had no need to embezzle money from anyone.

A deep disquiet settled within Sakina as she listened to Anjali's troubled words. Who was behind this venomous message, this attempt to tarnish Anjali's name and, by extension, their shared history? Hadn't they endured enough heartache already? This felt like a cruel twist of the knife, a shadowy figure determined to reopen old wounds and sow discord among them once more. The question hung heavy in the air: who was it who still sought to cast this evil shadow over the girls and their enduring friendship?

As Sakina listened to Anjali, her mind was a whirlwind. Adil's deteriorating state, Pam's suffocating presence, and now this disturbing development with Anjali. The weight of it all pressed down on her, making Ali's insistent demands feel like an unbearable burden. She knew he was right, that she couldn't keep postponing the inevitable. But the thought of delivering such a devastating blow to Adil in his fragile condition filled her with dread. The distance between them might be growing, but the fear of the finality of separation felt even more immense.

Chapter 29

Manish Gupta felt a knot of determination tighten in his chest. Kamal Gupta, his formidable father-in-law, saw him as little more than a bystander, a silent guardian of his Dubai-based music management company, Raagastar. The irony wasn't lost on Manish. He, a Gupta by marriage, relegated to the periphery while Rohit Jahangir, his business partner, confidently navigated the chaotic world of their artists. Rohit, it seemed, possessed an innate understanding of the current musical landscape, a landscape that frankly baffled Manish.

Hip-hop, R&B, Alternative Rock – the reigning genres of Gen Z – all sounded like noise to his ears without exception. He was not a musician, nor had he ever listened to this kind of music. He couldn't fathom the appeal. The glory days of MTV, of physical CD sales, were long gone, replaced by a generation that cherry-picked individual tracks, dismissing the concept of a cohesive album. Genuine talent, Manish believed, was drowning in a sea of fleeting TikTok trends. He remembered a time when album sales in their opening week would hit astronomical figures – half a million, a million, even two million. Now? The numbers were, as he saw it, dismal.

This decline in the traditional music industry only fuelled Manish's suspicion that something was amiss with Raagastar's finances. How was it possible that they were raking in such significant profits from their recently held concerts including the iconic Junoon tour? Manish was aware that ticket sales had fallen way beneath their estimates and there were barely any new artiste contracts signed by them.. Rohit – a smooth operator as always had dismissed his concerns. He had been at the helm for too long, while Manish remained the silent investor, a watchdog at Kamal Gupta's behest. Every time Manish had attempted to take a more active role, he'd been politely but firmly rebuffed by his father-in-law. The senior Mr. Gupta, a man steeped in generations of business acumen, clearly saw Rohit as the driving force of the business, the one worthy of his trust. "Stay on the sidelines, Manish," he'd advised, a directive that stung with each repetition. "Rohit knows what he is doing."

It felt like a profound slight. Manish was a Gupta now, having married Naina, Kamal's daughter. He had even set aside his own ambitions to join their family's enterprise. Surely, it was now his time to shine, to be recognised for his potential contribution. He wouldn't stand idly by any longer. He would delve into Raagastar's operations, dissect the financial statements, and unearth the truth. He would prove to Kamal Gupta that his son-in-law was not just a deadweight, but a sharp, vigilant businessman capable of safeguarding and even growing their shared legacy. The need to impress his father-in-law had morphed into a burning resolve to demonstrate his own capabilities, to finally step out of the shadows and into the light.

After months of skillfully dodging Manish's attempts at a face-to-face, Rohit had finally relented. The office, a neutral battleground of sorts, was where they would finally meet. Manish braced himself; pleasantries were unlikely. Years of friendship hadn't blinded him to Rohit's ruthlessness. If a shortcut to the summit of business success existed, Manish knew Rohit wouldn't hesitate to take it, ethics be damned.

Rohit was a flamboyant figure, a sharp shooter who aimed to win, consequences be damned. His casual disregard for business proprieties, his life's indiscretions, all bothered Manish deeply. "Don't take yourself so seriously, man!" Rohit would bellow, his laughter echoing through the Dubai Club during their boozy get-togethers. "I certainly don't." Manish often found himself reeling from this devil-may-care attitude, especially since it wasn't Rohit's own fortune he was playing with.

How had Rohit managed to charm the titans of the music industry and the deep-pocketed investors who were practically tripping over each other to pour money into his fledgling Raagastar? As far as Manish could tell, Rohit's secret weapon was his wife, Rupali. She was a true gem – dignified, ethereally beautiful, a woman of substance. Rupali and Manish had always shared an easy camaraderie, a quiet understanding. He knew she liked him. It perplexed Manish why women of such character were often drawn to men like Rohit Jahangir.

Over the past year, Manish had sensed a deep loneliness emanating from Rupali, a yearning for connection. Then the ugly whispers started – her rumoured affair with Avinash Batra, the vapid, toyboy husband of the socialite Ayesha Batra. Why would she stoop to that, Manish wondered, when she could have any man she desired? His thoughts drifted to his own life, a silent "what if" echoing in his mind. What if he had married Rupali instead of Naina, his perpetually critical wife who never let him forget that his very identity was tethered to her father's wealth?

The bitter truth was that Naina was right. Without the Gupta family's backing, Manish knew he'd likely be just another IIM graduate who'd arrived in Dubai years ago with ambitious dreams. Somewhere along the way, those dreams had morphed. Career ambition had faded, replaced by the allure of wealth and power. Marrying into the Gupta family had unlocked those doors. Somewhere in that transaction, Manish had bartered his sense of self-worth, his independence. But lately, that hardly seemed to matter anymore. The money and power more than made up for it.

Chapter 30

A cold fury, sharp and stinging like the desert wind, whipped through Rohit as he stormed out of the house. The roar of his Porsche Carrera engine sliced through the morning air as he merged onto Sheikh Zayed Road, the towering skyscrapers of downtown Dubai looming in the distance, mirroring his ambition and now, his simmering rage. Manish Gupta. The very name was a bitter taste on his tongue. The incessant, almost accusatory inquiries into Raagastar's books felt like a personal affront.

Of course, Rohit was acutely aware of the Gupta family's major stake in Raagastar. But it was *his* vision, *his* relentless drive, *his* innate understanding of the music industry that had propelled the company to its zenith. Who else could navigate the intricate melodies and discordant notes of this business with such finesse?

For years, Rohit had expertly "managed" Kamal Gupta, Manish's father-in-law, a seasoned tycoon whose vast portfolio often relegated Raagastar to a profitable, yet secondary concern. As long as the numbers sang a sweet tune, the senior Mr. Gupta rarely bothered to delve into the day-to-day operations. Investing in Raagastar had been more of a calculated gamble for him, a small chip on a much larger table.

Rohit remembered that day vividly. The nervous energy thrumming beneath his polished exterior as he waited for nearly three hours in their sterile office reception, while

Kamal Gupta concluded a call with his Korean partners. When finally granted a mere ten minutes, Rohit had seized the opportunity with both hands. He'd painted a vibrant picture of the Indian, UAE, and global music landscape, pinpointing untapped potential and articulating how Raagastar would revolutionise the Middle Eastern entertainment scene. It was a world alien to Mr. Gupta, a venture he would never have considered were it not for Rohit's compelling presence.

There was an undeniable spark about the young man that had intrigued Kamal Gupta. A fire in his eyes, a regal composure despite his supplicant stance. Above all, a palpable passion for music. A musician himself back in the day, Rohit possessed that rare alchemy of creative vision and business acumen. "It's got to work, Sir," he'd declared, his gaze unwavering, direct. "I know this industry inside out. I will not allow it to fail."

Against his better judgement, Mr. Gupta had succumbed to Rohit's relentless pursuit. The follow-up emails, the articles on global music giants, Rohit's persistent presence in Dubai's business circles – it was a campaign of unwavering conviction. Eventually, Kamal Gupta had invested 500,000 AED in a "friends and family" funding round, blissfully unaware that he was the sole significant contributor. "I will want a royalty as well," he'd stated, a businessman's instinct to protect his capital. "At least until I get my principal back."

Nothing could ruffle Rohit's feathers. He remained cool, composed, supremely confident. And over the years, he had delivered results, transforming Raagastar into the undisputed leader in Middle Eastern music and entertainment. "He's my blue-eyed boy," Gupta would often proclaim. "Brilliant boy. I trust him blindly. Always have and always will."

But the landscape had shifted. Kamal Gupta's health was now failing, and he had ceded operational control to Manish, his son-in-law. Rohit had known Manish for years – the sharp IIM graduate with those calculating brown eyes and an obsequious demeanour in his father-in-law's presence. Of course, Kamal Gupta would choose a son-in-law who wouldn't question his authority. But now, with the old lion weakened, Manish finally saw his chance to carve his own territory, to show Rohit who truly held the reins. And the cold fury gripping Rohit promised a confrontation as sharp and unforgiving as the Dubai sun.

Chapter 31

Sakina Nawaz, a girl whose rustic charm was a familiar sight in the bylanes of Hyderabad, possessed a beauty that often drew unwanted attention. Her dusky complexion, large almond-shaped eyes, and naturally full lips were features frequently lauded as classically Indian. At MBB university, the gazes of her male classmates were a constant source of discomfort, particularly for her parents. "Is this what we send you to college for?" her father would fume, often directing his frustration towards her mother, "Ammi has thoroughly spoilt Sakina. Why pursue a psychology degree if her aspirations lie in modelling?" Yet, beneath his reprimands lay a deep affection, and Sakina always found herself with the funds to indulge her keen eye for fashion.

Sakina possessed an innate understanding of fashion and design. She effortlessly curated outfits, pairing traditional kurtas and jeans with striking silver earrings. Her curiosity extended to Western styles, and secret excursions with friends often involved quick changes into skirts and crop tops. However despite her popularity amongst the boys of her local community, the familiar comfort of her life in Hyderabad soon felt stifling. The small circles and lifelong acquaintances began to chafe against her independent spirit, leading to increasing friction with her parents. Realising it was time to forge her own path, Sakina cleverly used the guise of career ambitions to escape the confines of her hometown. Promising to stay in touch and reassuring her parents with the detail of an all-women's hostel in Calcutta, she packed her suitcases, brimming with the latest fashion trends, and left her psychology degree certificate safely locked away. Hyderabad, for Sakina, was now firmly in the rearview mirror, her sights set on a much grander life in a bustling metropolis.

Six months into her new life, Sakina found herself working as a receptionist in a five-star hotel. Her CV was barely glanced at; the manager's focus was solely on her striking appearance. Sakina endured the uncomfortable interview, acutely aware of his gaze lingering on her. She had carefully chosen a modest white, full-sleeved top with a demure V-neck and a fitted green skirt, each garment accentuating her hourglass figure. "Thank you, the job is yours," the manager had said immediately after, adding softly as she left, "...you look very beautiful, madam...like a heroine!" The initial embarrassment and humiliation of constant advances from hotel guests gradually faded as Sakina's confidence grew. She proved to be not just alluring but remarkably intelligent, a combination that quickly earned her the praise of senior management. The psychology degree gathering dust back home was a distant memory. Her parents remained under the impression that she held a general management role, her mother's primary concern being marriage proposals and settling down.

One afternoon, as Sakina meticulously reviewed the hotel's room register, a quiet voice inquired, "Hello ma'am, do you have my reservation?" Adil Chaudhry was a man of unassuming appearance – square-faced, bespectacled, with a stocky build and neatly combed black hair. He could have been any other Indian man, unremarkable save for his eyes. They held a spark of keen intelligence, a curiosity that spoke of a man who had seen much of the world yet yearned to explore more. Discovering he was a senior banker with a prominent multinational firm, Sakina felt a surge of hope. She resolved to deploy her considerable charm and attentiveness towards Adil during his month-long stay. Adil, in turn, found himself captivated by Sakina's beauty and vivacious personality. Despite the likely disapproval of his conservative and affluent Bengali family, he was smitten. He knew he had to make her his.

Soon after the wedding he had received an offer to head a division of the prestigious ABQ bank in Dubai, United Arab Emirates. His parents were elated and broke many coconuts thanking the Lord for the blessings showered on their brilliant son. Sakina was used to being an outsider at their family celebrations. After all Adil's Ma and Baba had been horrified when he presented her in front of them as his new bride. Her own parents refused to have anything to do with her either. Inter-faith marriages were recipes for disaster in their opinion. Sakina stayed silent through it all. Perhaps they were destined to lead a life in Dubai after all, not amongst this constant family drama fighting their parents and their archaic beliefs. Adil adored her and in Dubai she would finally be free from the fetters of her past. She would reinvent herself as the glamorous wife of a wealthy banker. She had read about it so often in magazines and books feeding her imagination with myriad possibilities.

Life in Dubai unfolded like a dream for Sakina, each day a vibrant stroke on the canvas of her newfound happiness. Adil, true to his word, painted their days with the hues of her long-held desires. The moment they stepped into their centrally air-conditioned apartment in a swanky high-rise, a cool wave of relief washed over her, a stark contrast to the humid Indian air she was accustomed to. It felt like entering a different world, a world where comfort was not a luxury but a given.

Soon, a sleek, pearl-white sedan graced their driveway, its polished surface reflecting the dazzling Dubai sunlight. No more crowded trains or haggling with taxi drivers; now, Sakina could glide through the city in style, the gentle hum of the engine a soothing melody.

But it was the shopping that truly ignited a spark in Sakina's eyes. The sprawling malls, veritable palaces of consumerism, showcased a dazzling array of international brands and exquisite designs. Each visit felt like stepping into the pages of her beloved magazines, the possibilities as endless as her imagination had once conjured. She revelled in the freedom to choose, to adorn herself in ways she had only dreamt of before.

Adil watched her blossom in this new environment, his heart swelling with affection. He cherished the way her eyes sparkled with delight as she discovered new facets of Dubai, from the fragrant spice souks to the breathtaking views from the Burj Khalifa. He made sure their weekends were filled with exploration, from leisurely dinners at waterfront restaurants to thrilling desert safaris.

Sakina, in turn, embraced her role as the elegant wife of a successful banker. She cultivated a sophisticated style, her wardrobe a reflection of her newfound confidence. She learned to navigate the social circles of Dubai with grace, her innate warmth and intelligence shining through. The initial sting of her family's disapproval and her in-laws' coldness began to fade, replaced by the warmth of Adil's unwavering love and the excitement of their shared life.

Their apartment became a haven, filled with laughter and whispered secrets. Adil often held her close, tracing the delicate curve of her cheek, his eyes filled with adoration. "See, my Jaan," he would say softly, "Dubai is magical, just like you." And in his embrace, Sakina knew she had finally found her paradise, not just in a glittering city, but in the love of the man who had made all her dreams come true. She finally had her own home.

Chapter 32

The gleaming elevators of the Burj Khalifa whisked Rohit skyward, depositing him onto the 35th floor with a decisive *ding*. He strode out, his polished shoes clicking against the marble floor, each step a drumbeat of his mounting fury. Manish. The name tasted like ash in his mouth. Months he'd felt this storm brewing, the subtle shifts in Manish's demeanour, the probing questions about Raagastar's finances. Why else would the man, a peripheral figure at best, suddenly develop such a keen interest in the company's books?

Rohit's jaw tightened. Manish had contributed nothing to Raagastar's success, riding instead on the coattails of his father-in-law's favour. Publicly, he'd always echoed Kamal Gupta's praise for Rohit, a sycophantic echo. Now, the mask had slipped, revealing a weasel attempting a brazen takeover.

A familiar pang of frustration struck Rohit as he considered Naina. Kamal's own daughter, sharp-witted with degrees from Warwick and Bocconi, sidelined in favour of her husband. The strained dynamic between father and daughter, Kamal's dismissive attitude towards women in business – it had always been palpable. Rohit had noticed Rupali's growing closeness with Naina, a strategic alliance that smoothed his own path with the Guptas. He wondered if Naina had any idea of her husband's plans to oust him from Raagstar.

He offered a practiced smile to his receptionist, the pleasantry a stark contrast to the turmoil within. How was he going to navigate this? Manish was no fool, his education a clear advantage. Rohit would need every ounce of his cunning to paint his actions as being in Raagastar's best interest. But was Manish truly loyal to the Guptas? A question that hung in the air, unanswered.

"Hello buddy, good to see you man!" Manish's greeting was warm, a genuine echo of past camaraderie and being family friends for years. Rohit hoped this business conflict wouldn't shatter their connection. After a brief exchange of pleasantries, Rohit launched into an enthusiastic recount of his London trip, seamlessly transitioning to the upcoming wedding. "Rupali and I are just thrilled about Anisha and Karan Rawal," he announced, watching Manish's expression soften almost imperceptibly.

Rohit had always been acutely aware of Manish's quiet admiration for Rupali, the shared laughter, the deep conversations. It suited him to let that admiration simmer. After all Manish's own wife, Naina, was in a different league entirely. Manish, often treated as an afterthought in his own family, seemed to genuinely value the friendship he shared with Rohit & Rupali.

The steaming cups of coffee arrived, a momentary pause before the inevitable business discussion. Rohit, far from a novice, expertly parried Manish's initial inquiries, a smooth operator deflecting direct questions with vague pronouncements of "accountant errors" and convenient memory lapses regarding older transactions. He spun a complex web of half-truths about the intricacies of the music industry and the evolving nature of international artist contracts. He even introduced a note of veiled threat, warning of powerful figures who could jeopardise Raagastar's future if not handled with extreme caution.

Manish felt a creeping sense of disbelief. He'd come armed with a list of specific queries, yet Rohit effortlessly took control of the narrative, his professional demeanour and confident responses disarming.

"Who are these powerful people?" Manish finally asked, a cynical edge to his smile. "Friends or foes of Raagastar?"

"Well, that would depend, wouldn't it?" Rohit replied, a hint of mystery in his tone. *Would Nanam, the enigmatic Nadim Sheikh, Reva Rawal's so-called brother, be in his camp if Anisha married Karan?* The question hung unspoken in the air. Was securing his business empire worth sacrificing his daughter to a family with dubious connections?

Manish stared at Rohit, a knot of confusion tightening in his stomach. Who were these powerful individuals Rohit was entangled with, and what could they possibly have to do with Raagastar?

Manish eventually left with nothing. Rohit pushed their next review until after the board meeting three months away. Manish was well aware that every director on the board had witnessed his own father-in-law the doyen, Kamal Gupta allow Rohit to hold the reins of their operations several times in the past. It would be extremely difficult to make them believe anything to the contrary about Rohit Jahangir.

Manish knew he would have to tread carefully though. Rohit was clearly mixed up with some people who could hurt them hard if they put one step out of line.

When the doddering Kamal Gupta smiled at him vaguely as he got home, Manish smiled back sensing the questions on the old man's mind. " Just finished the review Papa. All good and your investment is in safe hands" It was all that the senior Mr. Gupta needed to hear as his nurse and his driver accompanied him outside for a drive to the Safa Park.

Chapter 33

Adjusting her baseball cap and staring blankly ahead, the young woman snarled into the phone, her voice laced with frustration. "She hasn't reacted to the messages the way you said she would." A month wasted in Dubai, so far from home, all for Dipika.

"She *will* call you for a meeting. Just keep pushing. There's too much money at stake, and that bitch Anjali knows exactly where it is. She's starting to sound rattled; I'm sure she's close to breaking."

A scoff escaped her lips. "She's not... I'm telling you. These people have so much money, they have no conscience. They lie to each other constantly, their relationships are meaningless, and they genuinely don't care about any accusations, okay? She's probably been called a cheat a million times."

The person on the other end of the line knew better. No one knew better than him the deep bond between Dipika and Anjali. She had been like a sister, a connection that had always grated on him, the extent of Dipika's trust in Anjali a constant irritation. Those final months had been tormented. Witnessing Dipika under the influence of substance abuse, perpetually stoned, unresponsive to his pleas.

Only he truly understood the agony of watching the woman he loved slip away while he remained trapped in another relationship. It was a tangled mess. Every attempt to reach Dipika had only pushed her further away, closer to Anjali. Of course, Anjali would have been oblivious to the fact that Dipika was his world, a secret they were both forced to carry. And yet, the cruellest blow was the depth of her hatred. Their life had become a charade. The group of friends – her so-called lifelines – had ultimately taken her life. They knew nothing of her true self and had left her utterly alone in her final days. He blamed himself, undoubtedly, but also those bitches whose lives had continued seamlessly after his darling's death. They deserved to suffer as he did, if not more. But revenge... revenge was imminent.

"I've got to go back home. Can't keep doing this shit forever can I?" She sometimes wondered how she had got taken in by his words. Dubai felt horribly alien to her and she was sick of constantly lurking in the shadows like this. She had never truly belonged anywhere and no place had ever felt like home. Suddenly the tears began to stream down her cheeks. Tears for all that she had loved and lost.

Chapter 34

Detective Razi Shufa of the Dubai Police, a man whose sharpness was often likened to a freshly honed blade and whose vigilance never wavered while on duty, found himself wrestling with a disquieting call. It had been over a year since he had successfully untangled the tragic mystery surrounding Dipika Luthra, the young Indian girl whose demise had gripped Dubai. That case was closed, the perpetrator brought to justice. Yet, the unexpected call from Adil Chaudhry had stirred a pool of unease within him.

Adil claimed he had seen Dipika. The very notion seemed impossible. Dead was dead, wasn't it? "These Indians," Razi mused, a touch of cultural generalisation colouring his thoughts, "always have some drama, their 'tamasha'." He had, in fact, kept a loose eye on the key players from the Luthra case. Adil and Sakina Chaudhry had returned to Dubai. The undeniably haughty Rohit and Rupali Jahangir continued their opulent existence in their sprawling villa, seemingly untouched by the past. Rohit's rapid ascent to wealth had always lingered in the back of Razi's mind – those meteoric rises in Dubai's corporate landscape often warranted a closer look.

But on that day, it had been Adil's frantic call that dominated his thoughts. Abrupt, breathless, his voice raw as if strained through a parched throat, Adil had uttered the unbelievable. "How is this possible, Mr. Chaudhry?" Razi had asked, a suspicion of intoxication or drug use clouding his judgement. The man had sounded utterly unhinged.

"Listen, Inspector," Adil had insisted, his voice laced with a desperate urgency. "I didn't have my specs. I can't *confirm* it, but I'm pretty sure it was her. In fact, I'm..." The line had gone dead, leaving Razi in a state of bewildered frustration. Who had Adil Chaudhry seen? The deceased did not simply reappear. Could it have been a lookalike? Despite repeated attempts, Adil's phone remained unanswered.

Razi Shufa thrived on puzzles. A skilled Crime Scene Investigator as well as a seasoned detective, he relished the intricate dance of unravelling complex mysteries. The more convoluted the truth, the more determined he became. He had proven that in the Luthra case. Popping a succulent, walnut stuffed date into his mouth, he chewed thoughtfully. *One lie is enough to question all truths.* The question that gnawed at him was: which of Dipika's friends was now weaving a deception, and for what reason?

His pursuit of Adil Chaudhry led him to a grim discovery. Mr. Chaudhry had suffered a massive head injury and lay unconscious. What crucial piece of information had he been on the verge of revealing just before he fell? Detective Shufa then turned his attention to Anjali Sen...Dipika's closest friend and ally. Her responses were unusually vague, her demeanour evasive. He sensed a hidden truth lurking beneath her carefully constructed facade. "Is everything alright, Ms. Sen?" he inquired, his voice laced with genuine concern. "Yes, of course, Inspector," she replied, a subtle tremor betraying her forced composure.

Something is definitely wrong, Razi concluded, a familiar thrill of investigation coursing through him. *It's time to open up the Luthra case files again.*

Chapter 35

He said *what*, Mom? Oh my God, I can't believe it! What fantastic news, Ma!" Anisha's voice bubbled with a joy that sent a wave of relief through Rupali. After their trip to London and the rather peculiar encounter with Karan's family, particularly his eccentric Uncle Nanam, Anisha had been so subdued. Rupali had sensed her daughter's unease, the worry that Karan's parents hadn't fully embraced the match.

Then Rohit had burst into their bedroom, his enthusiasm a stark contrast to the earlier quiet. "Let's move the engagement forward, babe! There's no need for us to wait after all. Speak to Reva and ask them to fly down to Dubai. We'll host a really classy dinner and arrange it however she wants. I want my princess to have the wedding of her dreams!"

Rupali, though surprised by his sudden eagerness, was undeniably delighted. She had felt a collective dip in their excitement after the London trip, especially concerning Nanam – Nadim Sheikh, Karan's uncle. But seeing the sheer happiness radiating from Anisha now made all those worries fade into insignificance. Hearing her daughter's voice, so light and full of joy after what felt like ages, confirmed they were doing the right thing. Anisha genuinely loved Karan, and Rupali could finally envision the beautiful future her daughter dreamt of and so fully deserved.

Unknown to both his wife and daughter, Rohit harboured a secret motive for his newfound enthusiasm. A clandestine phone call with Nadim Sheikh – Nanam – had sealed his decision. "We are friends now, Mr. Jahangir," Nanam had stated, his voice carrying a peculiar weight. "What are you thinking so hard about? Reva is my sister, and Karan is her only son. If he wants to marry your daughter – he will. You know that I will do anything for family. I'm sure you will too… no?" Rohit had found himself speechless, agreeing quickly.

His company, Raagastar, was facing a threat from Manish Gupta's attempted takeover, leaving Rohit on precarious ground. He had poured his life into building Raagastar's success. While the whispers among Dubai's elite circles were unsettling, they didn't truly worry him. With Nanam – Nadim Sheikh – as his ally, he would become a formidable force in the business world. Even Manish Gupta would think twice before challenging him. Nanam had assured him his visit to Dubai would be brief, just to bless the young couple, a detail that suited Rohit perfectly.

Yes, things were finally falling into place. For all the rumours that painted him as a devil in disguise, Rohit now had a devil by his side. And perhaps, he mused, that wasn't such a bad thing after all.

Rupali's fingers trembled slightly as she dialled Reva Rawal's number. Each ring felt like a tiny drumbeat against her already frayed nerves. She clutched her phone tightly, rehearsing the opening lines in her head, her mind a whirl of engagement plans, wedding dates, and the sheer logistics of it all, especially in Dubai.

"Hello?" Reva's voice was crisp, as Rupali had always known it.

Taking a deep breath, Rupali began, her tone carefully formal. "Namaste, Mrs. Rawal. This is Rupali… Anisha's mother. I wanted to discuss the engagement…"

"Of course, Rupali," Reva's voice interjected, surprisingly warm and devoid of its usual formality. "Please, call me Reva. We're practically family now, aren't we? And we all love Anisha. Such a lovely girl."

Rupali blinked, taken aback by the other woman's friendly tone. This wasn't the reserved and somewhat intimidating Reva she had anticipated.

"Nanam Bhai gave his blessings too," Reva continued, her tone genuinely pleased. "In fact, he just called me to say he wants us to go ahead. The children's happiness is our happiness too. Rishabh will be okay with whatever we decide. We are simple people."

Rupali was truly bewildered. It was almost as if she was talking to a different person. What had happened to change Reva's attitude this dramatically?

"And Dubai for the engagement sounds perfect, dear," Reva added readily. "After all, that is where Anisha spent her childhood, and it's home to her."

Whatever it was that had caused the change in Reva's attitude, Rupali was truly relieved. A wave of lightness washed over her. Now they could finally plan the engagement without the anticipated hurdle. She could already picture the celebrations.

Her mind immediately jumped to her friends. She'd round up the girls to help her plan the event. Sakina seemed more cheerful now that Adil was at least at home, even if he was on a wheelchair. Naina had promised Rupali she would lend her invaluable assistance too. She did have the most envied blackbook with some of the most exclusive catering and decor contacts in town.

It was only Anjali that Rupali was seriously worried about. She seemed vague and distracted every time Rupali tried to speak to her and refused to tell any of them what was bothering her. When Rupali had texted her to check if the strange WhatsApp messages to her from "Dipika" had stopped, Anjali had replied with a curt, one-word answer: "YES!" Something told Rupali that her friend was lying to her. If she wasn't this distracted herself, Rupali would have enquired further, but hey… the Jahangirs were going to be planning a wedding! A joyous occasion that deserved all her attention.

Chapter 36

Sakina's journey to becoming a prominent beauty and fashion influencer in Dubai unfolded quite unexpectedly. The initial spark ignited with a simple photoshoot outside the iconic Tiffany Blue, captured by a keen-eyed photographer for their inaugural promotional campaign. The resulting images possessed an undeniable allure, a certain "earthy sensuality" that resonated deeply with both the producers and the client.

The photographer's subsequent email, requesting a professional portfolio shoot, came as a delightful shock to Sakina. Her cautious inquiry about payment was met with an enthusiastic confirmation, along with the promising words, "You are going to be a very busy lady." This marked the pivotal moment where Sakina's innate grace and style began their transformation into a burgeoning career.

Later that evening, the arrival of two large suitcases at her doorstep felt like a dream. Inside lay a treasure trove of high fashion – exquisite clothes from Lanvin and Emilio Pucci, coveted Chanel bags, and elegant dresses from Diane Von Furstenberg. These were the very brands she had admired during her window-shopping excursions in Dubai's luxurious malls. The sheer reality of these items being hers to wear for a photoshoot was almost unbelievable.

Sharing this exciting development with her husband, Adil, filled their home with joy. Adil, on his path to recovery, had become increasingly aware of his cousin Pamela's subtle condescension towards Sakina for not having a traditional career. Pamela's remarks about financial independence stung, especially as Adil now perceived her corporate success as masking a deeper loneliness and a need for control. He was genuinely thrilled to see Sakina reconnecting with her long-held passion for fashion, recognising her natural talent for modelling and her inherent sense of style. The fact that she would now be paid for it was an added bonus.

From her very first professional shoot, Sakina shone effortlessly. Her natural ability in front of the camera translated into captivating images, leading to a steady stream of engagements. With each project, her confidence grew, and her unique charm radiated through the photographs and videos she created. Before long, her online presence flourished and her followers multiplied rapidly, drawn to her authentic style and captivating persona. And suddenly just like that, Sakina, the ordinary woman who had once simply posed for a snapshot outside a café, had firmly established herself as a sought-after beauty and fashion influencer in the dazzling world of Dubai.

Anjali was thrilled at the developments as were Rupali & Naina ..." Sakina ", I can hardly believe it said Naina. I mean...she had such a typically Indian vibe earlier...of course she carries herself with so much confidence now and looks fabulous," she quickly added not wanting to sound bitchy.

Staring at her first pay check, Sakina had to pinch herself to believe that people would actually pay that much for her photographs. As she quickly amassed over 350,000 followers she earned 10,000 AED for every post. Her captions were witty and fun and her pictures were sensational. She learned how to create stories, how to shoot reels and influence the buying behaviour of her followers. And most of all she was having a lot of fun!

Her dreams had finally come true and she was learning what it felt like to wield power and influence of her own.

When Ali Rez called her from London to catch up with her, she was in the middle of a shoot. She did pause however to take the call and tell him to get lost. She was done with being manipulated and threatened. Adil and her had found their peace again and there was no one who could take it away from them.

Hanging up, she didn't get to hear the rest of Ali's foul abuses. However she had no doubt that he would find another Sakina somewhere.. Men like him usually did, which was the tragedy of it all.

Chapter 37

Unbeknownst to her other friends, Anjali had called Adil one afternoon, timing it perfectly for when Sakina was away on a shoot. She knew Adil was recovering well, and perhaps now was the opportune moment to ask if he had truly seen Dipika. The specific details in each WhatsApp message convinced her that this wasn't just a random prank. Adil answered on the first ring.

"Anjali, what a pleasant surprise! You should have come over for tea; it's been ages, my friend," he chuckled. "Despite whatever Sakina might have told you, I'm doing much better."

"That's wonderful to hear, Adil. I've been meaning to visit for a while. Let's plan something soon. Actually, I just had a quick question for you, if you don't mind."

"Shoot," Adil replied, his voice calm and steady.

"Adil, do you recall the other day at the hospital, when I was there with you? You mentioned seeing Dipika." Anjali's voice grew urgent. "You seemed so certain. Adil, this is really important to me. I'm at my wit's end. Can you please try and remember if you saw her?"

A long silence stretched from the other end of the line, broken only by Adil's deep breaths. She knew he hadn't hung up.

"Adil... please try to remember. It's important. Did you see Dipika? Do you remember where?"

Adil…you of all people know the truth. I had shared everything with you, the bank statements, the remittances. You have to help me here. Whoever has contacted me is obviously not Dipika but someone else attempting to blackmail me.

This money trail …you remember what she had asked me to do? …Anjali broke off wondering if Adil was still on the line.

"Who is Dipika?" he finally responded, his voice devoid of emotion. "Anjali, when will you come and visit me? Please come and see me. I get lonely."

Promising to visit him soon, Anjali quickly ended the call. Adil's recent neuro-surgery had clearly affected his memory; there was no doubt about that. She couldn't risk asking him anything further. She would have to find her own answers.

Sitting far away in the headquarters of the Dubai Police, Detective Razi Shufa prided himself that the UAE had one of the most advanced surveillance systems in the world, which included all online modes as real life monitoring of public spaces.

Mr. Adil Chaudhry's phones had been under surveillance, ever since he had been discharged from the hospital. It was now apparent that Anjali Sen had some secrets of her own that she did not want to reveal. But why was she hiding this information and from whom?

Adil Chaudhry had clearly been her confidante in this matter. How very sad that he should have now suffered this retrograde amnesia after his recent accident.

Sometimes, a tiny quirk of fate can turn the entire course of an investigation, thought Detective Shufa as he played the recording again and again.

Adil Chaudhary may have lost his memory but not before he had called the Inspector that fateful morning of his accident and he had sounded very sure about whom he had seen.

The Inspector thought carefully about that. Obviously it was not Dipika Luthra – back from the dead but then... who could it be?

Relishing a piece of Luqaimat – the delicious dough ball drizzled with sugar syrup after his lunch that afternoon, it suddenly struck him.

Only two people were the co-accused in the criminal investigation into Ms. Luthra's demise, and one of them, of course, was languishing in jail.

There was only one other person who knew as much about Dipika Luthra as Anjali Sen did.

Deported from the UAE as the result of his conviction, they had all paid scant regard to what he was upto these days in Africa. Perhaps it was time to pay an overdue visit to an old friend.

Chapter 38

In the meanwhile, Anjali had decided to take matters into her own hands. She was sick of being the victim of this emotional blackmail and vendetta.

Having never dared to reply to the WhatsApp messages, she now decided to respond to the latest one received the previous evening.

"Anjali...I'm done with your games. You cheated me, and we both know it. Wire the money to the account as per the details I'm giving you. "You have 48 hours, babe, or I'll be happy to let our darling friends know you are a bloody cheat – the worst kind!"

"Come and see me at home, Dippy, Anjali calmly typed. It's been too long."

She sat down in her dimly lit drawing room and stared at the wall calmly, waiting for her phone to ping with a notification.

Sitting in her apartment in the Dubai Marina, her tormentor was furiously making a phone call.

"That's it. I'm done. This bitch Anjali knows nothing about any money. She has nerves of steel. Asking me to come home. You should never have got me involved with these women. Dipika was crazy to pick them as her friends... to trust them this much! Maybe there is no money after all and she's run through it." she ranted.

She had wasted so much time in Dubai, chasing this pipe dream and hoping to go back home rich. But the money wasn't coming near her …anytime soon.

Far away in Africa, Rakesh Rai listened to her ranting without saying much. He had no option. Sitting in front of him was Police Detective Razi Shufa. He knew his game was up.

At Anjali's end, the messages had suddenly stopped and Anjali wondered how her blackmailer had suddenly given up. A call from a familiar voice interrupted her thoughts the next morning.

"Ms. Anjali Sen – it is such a pleasure madam. You have forgotten me but I will not forget you." Its Inspector Razi Shufa from the Dubai Police.

May I request you to kindly come down to the station this afternoon.

Chapter 39

The Dubai heat seemed to amplify Anjali's already frayed nerves. Traffic had been relentless, each delay a fresh spike of anxiety. By the time she finally navigated the imposing, sand-coloured facade of the police headquarters, she was a mess of sweat, worry, and simmering panic. She'd barely slept, replaying Dipika's last words, Rakesh's accusations, and the gnawing uncertainty of what awaited her.

She rushed through the lobby, her footsteps echoing in the vast, cool space, and after a few hurried questions to a disinterested officer, she found herself outside the investigation room. Taking a deep, shaky breath, she pushed the door open.

The scene inside was… unexpected.

Detective Razi Shufaa, a man with sharp, observant eyes and an aura of quiet authority, sat at a steel table. That much was as she'd pictured. But beside him sat a woman who was the spitting image of Dipika!

Same striking features, same confident posture, same… everything. Except, there was a subtle hardness in this woman's gaze, a certain edge that Dipika never possessed.

Anjali froze, her mind reeling. *Dipika? But… how?*

Detective Shufaa's voice cut through her stunned silence. "Ms. Anjali, please, come in. This is Simran. Dipika's twin sister."

Twin sister? The words hung in the air, heavy with disbelief. Anjali's head swam. Mansi aunty had *never* mentioned a twin. Never. It was as if a crucial piece of Dipika's life, a whole other person, had been deliberately erased.

Simran's expression was unreadable. "So, you're Anjali," she said, her voice cool and measured. "Dipika spoke of you very often." There was no warmth in her tone, only a detached curiosity.

Anjali, still reeling, managed a weak nod. She couldn't process this. Dipika had a twin? And she was here?

Detective Shufaa gestured to a chair. "Please, sit down, Ms. Anjali. We have a few things to discuss." He watched Anjali closely, his expression serious. He knew this revelation would shake things up.

The detective knew that Simran had lived in Sao Paulo, Brazil, for years, on her own terms. She'd left home at 17 after running away from college with a boyfriend, a move that had brought "disgrace" to her family, leading Mansi aunty to essentially erase her from their history. Dipika and Simran had maintained occasional contact, a strong sibling bond persisting despite the distance and family estrangement. Rakesh Rai ofcourse was obsessed with Dipika. He was the only one who knew about Simran, and he had tracked her down, after Dipika's demise.

Of course YOU were the only person Dipika told about her family fortune Ms. Anjali. You were the only one she really trusted and Rakesh couldn't stand that. She was the one, after all who asked you to take control of her finances, to send the money for her mother's medical bills. She was deeply worried about the onset of her mother, Mansi Luthra's early dementia.

And most of all, she wanted you to keep quiet about all of this. Noone needed to know. Yes you kept your friend's secret even beyond the grave Ms, Anjali as only a true friend will do. You didn't even tell me but then of course it is my job to find out!

At this point, Simran began to softly weep. "I was wrong …so wrong about you."

I miss her so much Anjali. Dippy had been there for me right through. Even after my parents kicked me out and then pretended I did not exist. She was the only one who truly loved me. "

I'm sorry … He played me …I really believed Rakesh when he said you had frauded my sister. That's why.. I mean I came to Dubai and sent you those….her voice tapered off choked with emotion.

Anjali could barely respond. Just watching Simran in front of her felt as if Dipika was back. They looked so similar. Despite herself and the curious gaze of the Police detective, Anjali hugged Simran. The police would take care of the rest. The nightmare had finally ended.

Chapter 40

The Jahangir family engagement party was undeniably the talk of Dubai, a shimmering testament to exquisite taste and familial joy. Rupali and Rohit orchestrated a truly unforgettable evening for their daughter Anisha at Rasa, the coveted beachfront jewel. Within the private dining room, an air of refined elegance reigned supreme. The tables were adorned with delicate blooms and sparkling crystal, enveloped by the luxurious embrace of handwoven silk furnishings, tapestries, and brocades – a masterpiece crafted by a discerning event decorator.

Staying true to the Rawals' preference for intimacy, the Jahangirs curated an exclusive guest list of just thirty individuals for this highly anticipated soiree. Sakina, Rupali, Anjali, and Naina poured their hearts into realising Anisha's dream engagement, and their efforts yielded a truly fabulous affair.

Rasa's heavy oak doors swung inward with a soft whoosh everytime a guest arrived.

As Sakina entered, a ripple of stunned silence spread through the small gathering of friends. It wasn't just the dress, though the crimson Balenciaga, a sculpted masterpiece of silk and daring angles, certainly commanded attention. It clung to her frame with an effortless grace, the vibrant red a bold declaration in itself.

But it was more than the dress. It was the way she carried herself. Gone was the hesitant slump of her shoulders, the downcast gaze she used to favour. This Sakina moved with a fluid confidence, her chin held high, her eyes meeting theirs with a steady, knowing light. Each step she took across the polished floor was deliberate, radiating an inner strength they hadn't witnessed before.

The moment Sakina graced the venue, a ripple of excitement went through the room. Instantly recognisable as one of Dubai's latest social media influencers in beauty and fashion, she was met with a flurry of admiring glances. Adil allowed her to stride in ahead of him, while he lagged behind. She had waited too long for her place in the limelight. Her time had finally come.

A soft smile played on her lips as she greeted each of her admirers, her voice a little deeper, imbued with a newfound resonance. Her presence spoke volumes. Her friends saw it in the assured curve of her smile, the easy laughter that punctuated her stories, the decisive way she offered her opinion on a topic of discussion.

This wasn't the Sakina who had once shrunk into the background, unsure of her place. This was a woman who knew her worth, who had embraced her power. The transformation wasn't just external; it was etched in the very fabric of her being. As she effortlessly navigated the conversation, a vibrant energy surrounding her, her friends exchanged knowing glances. The girl they once knew had blossomed into a woman who owned her space, radiant and undeniably transformed.

Nearby, Naina Gupta sat beside her husband, Manish. His composed expression offered no hint of the tense conversation that had transpired at home earlier. Naina, well aware of Manish's ongoing investigation into the Raagastar books had chosen this moment to deliver a significant announcement. With a quiet resolve, she informed him of her formal appointment to the Board of Directors. Manish had no insight into these recent developments. It was a fait accompli – as Kamal Gupta's only daughter, she felt it was her duty to safeguard his legacy. Who could challenge that. She requested that Manish "toe the line" and cease his inquiries into Rohit's affairs. She conveyed her implicit trust in him, echoing her father's faith. She would need Rohit's help to understand the business better. Left with little recourse, Manish offered a subtle nod of agreement. There was simply no other choice. Rohit had won again!

A vision of ethereal beauty, Anisha then entered, her radiant smile illuminating the room. She was accompanied by her fiancé, Karan, and his parents, the Rawals. Her peach and white chiffon tulle dress was adorned with a delicate hand-embroidered lace border crafted by Reva's grandmother and perfectly captured her joy at this alliance. Rohit and Rupali beamed with pride, their hearts swelling at the sight of their daughter's happiness. A wave of relief washed over Rohit as he noted the absence of Karan's controversial uncle, "Nanam," who, despite not attending the engagement in person, had sent a magnificent bouquet of flowers, a dazzling diamond bracelet from Tiffany's Bridal collection for Anisha, and a stunning pair of Cartier earrings for Rupali.

Anjali arrived shortly after, accompanied by Abhay and Simran, who had been staying with her. Over the past weeks, Simran had come to understand just how much of a support Anjali had been to her sister and was deeply grateful to have her presence in her own life.

As Adil made his entrance, finally able to walk with the aid of a cane, it became sadly obvious that the accident had left its mark, on his memory. Sakina had vowed to never leave him though and that was all he cared about. As Anjali offered a polite introduction to Simran, Dipika's twin sister, he politely shook her hand without a flicker of recognition.

As they watched him from across the room, Rupali and Sakina exchanged a knowing glance, a silent acknowledgement of the strength and resilience of their enduring friendship, through thick and thin. That was literally all that mattered on this day.

As the breathtaking Dubai sunset painted the sky in hues of gold and rose, Anjali, Rupali, Naina, and Sakina raised a silent toast to one another and to new beginnings. A testament to their bond and the beautiful celebration they had brought to life. The Jahangir engagement party was more than just a gathering; it was a moment etched in the social fabric of Dubai, a dazzling affair that would be fondly remembered for a long time to come.

Somehow they all felt it was the harbinger of many more celebrations together in this beautiful city of Dubai, their home away from home.

The End.

www.ingramcontent.com/pod-product-compliance
Lightning Source LLC
Chambersburg PA
CBHW031039160726
47991CB00005B/1947